"D

"To what?" I squeaked, ruining Tina's solemn ceremony. My voice was sounding ultra high for some reason. Maybe because I was nervous.

Tina sounded exasperated with me again. "Just say yes, Jendra!" she exclaimed with a sigh. "It isn't that hard!"

"Okay," I said, feeling dumb. "Yes."

"If you betray our secret, Death will seize your soul!" she finished spookily.

"Hey," I yelped. "That's severe. You didn't tell me a threat like that was coming, or I might not have said yes."

"Just shut up and everything will be fine," Tina assured me shortly.

We ran out of water just about then, so Tina pulled our raft over to the bank, and we got out on a tiny piece of ground. There wasn't much room to stand, and it was still really dark. In fact, all I could see was a big green door, at least three times as tall as I was, with big brass bolts all over it. I didn't know what was beyond the door, but something must have been pretty hot there because steam was spraying out all along the sides.

I cocked an eyebrow suspiciously. "What is this?" I demanded. "The door to Hell or something?"

"Close," said Tina, which wasn't very reassuring. With much less effort than I would have expected, she tapped on the door three times in the middle and it opened up.

Suddenly I was met with the shock of my life. . . .

Night
of the
Pompon

Sarah Jett

AN ARCHWAY PAPERBACK
Published by POCKET BOOKS

New York   London   Toronto   Sydney   Singapore

This book is a work of fiction. Names, characters, places, and incidents are products of the author's imagination or are used fictitiously. Any resemblance to actual events or locales or persons, living or dead, is entirely coincidental.

AN ARCHWAY PAPERBACK *Original*

An Archway Paperback published by
POCKET BOOKS, a division of Simon & Schuster, Inc.
1230 Avenue of the Americas, New York, NY 10020

Copyright © 2000 by Sarah J. Jett

ISBN: 0-671-78633-4

First Archway Paperback printing October 2000

10 9 8 7 6 5 4 3 2

AN ARCHWAY PAPERBACK and colophon are registered trademarks of Simon & Schuster, Inc.

Front cover illustration by Bill Schmidt

Printed in the U.S.A.

IL 6+

For my little sister Merry
(the best Christmas present Mom and Dad ever
gave me)

1
The Floating Legs

Night lasts a long time when it's winter in Antarctica.

But, unfortunately, I live in Texas, so I never get enough sleep.

Because of this, I frequently have delusions. I think I can do all kinds of crazy, superhuman things.

Like take pre-algebra instead of regular seventh-grade math.

Believe me, that was just about the biggest mistake I'd ever made. I don't know what I was thinking! My counselor told me, "Jendra, your placement test results are extremely high. I think you can test into Mrs. O'Donnahee's pre-algebra class." *And then she gave me a peanut-butter cup.* So what could I do?

"I think you'll enjoy the challenge," she said.

And I was like, "Okay!"

Ughhhhhhhhhhhhhhhhhhhhhhh.

So there I was, sitting at the back of the class one muggy Wednesday morning at about 8 A.M., staring at the equation on the overhead and thinking, *That is so fascinating!*

Mrs. O'Donnahee makes little lines through her sevens just like I do! Isn't that just too, too cool? I call them my Eurosevens.

Now, as for the equation . . .

$$7x + 3 = 24$$

I stared at it for a very long time. Like five minutes. Until the numbers started to move around and change places. Mrs. O'Donnahee was explaining something about "isolating variables." But I hadn't done any homework for about three weeks, so I had absolutely no idea what she was talking about.

$$7x + 3 = 24$$

I stared at it again. This time I concentrated really hard. Suddenly I had an epiphany!

(My mom's an English teacher, so I like to throw around literary terms.) An *epiphany,* in case you don't know, is a burst of deep, amazing truth in a sudden brilliant, blinding flash.

So I had an epiphany. And I knew . . .

I am never going to understand algebra!

Well, as you can imagine, that was a pretty big relief because then I didn't have to waste my time trying anymore. I was free to stare out the window and doodle on my paper. Eurosevens are great for starting up a game of hangman, by the way.

The only problem is, hangman isn't the most entertaining game to play by yourself. In fact, you pretty much *can't* play by yourself.

So, after about two minutes of trying, I was getting really bored.

I knew I needed something else to do. I needed some plan of action, some way to escape. Something daring. Something thrilling . . .

"Mrs. O'Donnahee," I said, raising my hand at the same time, "can I go to the bathroom?"

Mrs. O'Donnahee glared back at me wickedly, her pupils lit up like smoldering coals. "No!" she screamed. "Never! *Never! Never!*"

Okay, so that didn't really happen. I just figured that since I'm writing a book and everything, I should at least try to make it interesting and use all that stuff you learn about in language arts—you know, similes, conflict.

Of course, Mrs. O'Donnahee let me go to the bathroom. I mean, I live in *Texas,* not *Siberia!*

Have you ever noticed that the halls are really quiet during class? I guess that's because there's nobody in them, duh! But, I mean, it's so quiet it's almost eerie. It's like you're walking through a ghost town, and you're the only person left alive. Or like you're escaping from a mental institution or something.

Or maybe I'm just weird. Who knows.

But the point is, as I walked through the empty halls to the bathroom, I had the strangest feeling that something really, really weird was about to happen.

Of course, I always have that feeling. I think it's because I'm bored a lot, and I just really *want* something to happen. And then, sometimes, I get lucky, and something actually does happen.

And that day was one of those times because as soon as I stepped into the bathroom, I noticed that something was seriously wrong. I had the eeriest sensation that I wasn't alone in there. Then, as I was shutting the stall door, I happened to look up and see two legs dangling above my head.

I thought that was a little unusual, especially since it was a girls' bathroom, and the legs were wearing pressed khaki slacks and men's loafers. In fact, as the legs started moving higher and higher up, one of the shoes slipped off and fell into the toilet. Meanwhile, the legs floated away, up and out of sight. For the first time I noticed that one of the white ceiling panels had been removed. That was how the legs had made their grand exit—through the square hole in the ceiling. As soon as the legs disappeared completely, the ceiling panel mysteriously slipped back into place. Good-bye, legs. Good-bye, hole. Good-bye, hall pass.

I say "good-bye, hall pass" because while I was craning my neck, staring at the ceiling like a big moron, I accidentally dropped Mrs. O'Donnahee's paper hall pass into the toilet, too.

I winced. *Good thing it's laminated,* I thought as I reached into the toilet bowl to snatch back the pass and fish out the shoe. A split second later, holding the drippy shoe and the slick pass in my wet hand, I suddenly felt a wave of utter ickiness.

I tried to fix things by setting the shoe on the toilet paper dispenser and rinsing my hands off *(in the sink),* but that didn't really help. Now that the legs were gone, I was just stuck with that stupid shoe. And I didn't have a clue what to do with it. Actually, I didn't know what to do at all. Going to the bathroom suddenly seemed kind of anticlimactic. Know what I mean? And what else can a person really do in a bathroom?

After thinking about it a minute, I decided that the best plan was to sit on the bathroom counter and stare at the shoe until I figured out what was going on. Now, that may not sound like such a great plan, but think about it this way—my runner-up plan was to go back to class.

Why would some guy's legs be floating up through the ceiling? I asked myself. The first answer that came to mind was alien abduction. Gee, I wonder why! Maybe because every single thing in bookstores, and on posters, and on TV, and in the movies now is about aliens? My friend Leah keeps telling me that people who believe in aliens are just stupid and immature (like me). But whenever anyone brings up the subject of aliens invading the Earth, she suddenly gets real quiet and starts to tremble a little. Leah scares easily.

Personally, I'm not expecting an extraterrestrial invasion anytime soon. I mean, sure, sometimes, I think it might be kind of *fun* if aliens came to our school. I don't really know what we would do exactly if they did, but I'm pretty sure it wouldn't be pre-algebra, and that's a good enough start for me.

But in the meantime, I couldn't quite bring myself to believe that aliens had abducted some guy from a stall of a second-story girls' bathroom. Even though that would have really been cool.

SARAH JETT

It's easy, and even kind of fun to believe in all kinds of mythical creatures and extraterrestrial beings. But, really, most events, no matter how weird they seem, actually have a very normal, rational, humanly possible explanation. And to me, that's what's really amazing and really scary. People do some pretty weird stuff for some pretty strange reasons. People you think you know. People who know you.

Who pulled those legs through the bathroom ceiling? I didn't know then. But I do know now. And the way I found out had a lot to do with the crumpled piece of pompon I found stuck to the bottom of the soggy shoe.

2
Tina

For a long time I really wanted to live in Paris so I could go to a sidewalk café and eat lunch on the banks of the Rhine. Then my dad told me the Rhine was in Germany. But it doesn't really matter because I can't speak French anyway, so this whole fantasy really doesn't make much sense. I just like the idea of eating croissants outside in the sunshine and ordering lunch from a waiter with a little mustache and a lopsided beret.

Eating in the cafeteria just isn't the same. I mean, the lunch monitor lady does have a little mustache, but the similarities stop there. Sad but true.

I was already sitting at our usual table when my best friend, Leah Livingston, glided over to sit beside me. Leah's been my best friend since fourth grade, and in all those years she's never really changed. She's one of those people who likes to do absolutely everything by the rules all the time. And she expects everyone else to be just as perfect as she is; otherwise she throws whiny little fits. It gets annoying sometimes, but I guess it's not her fault. Her mom's real overprotective. And Leah's pretty, so people put up with her.

As soon as Leah put her tray down on the table, I set the shoe down next to it.

Leah cocked an eyebrow. "Jendra," she said with a grin, trying to be funny, "are you dieting again?"

"I found this in the bathroom," I told her bluntly.

"You're amazing," said our mutual friend Matthew Greyson, plunking down in the seat on my other side. "I can never find shoes I like!" Matt and Leah and I always hang around together, but we're just friends. People never believe that, but that's too bad.

"Why did you bring that *thing* to the table?" Leah demanded. The shoe *was* pretty grungy-looking. I'll give her that. She gave it the evil eye and tried to protect her pizza from it by moving it to the far side of her tray.

"Because I found it in the toilet," I said. It seemed pretty obvious to me.

Leah didn't say anything. She just gave me a look.

"What?" I demanded. "What's wrong with that?"

Matt said with a wicked smile, "I'm surprised you didn't find a whole outfit. You were in the bathroom for like twenty-five minutes." He swept his auburn hair back out of his eyes and took out a deck of Magic cards to entertain himself while he waited for the line to go down. "But, really, though, what's up with the shoe?"

I smiled slowly and explained, "I've been trying to figure out whose it is."

Suddenly Matt surprised me by yelling, "Mine!" He grabbed the shoe and shoved it on his foot. "There," he said triumphantly. "It fits. Now can we get married and live happily ever after?"

"Don't wear that shoe!" Leah exclaimed in horror, wrinkling her nose in disgust. Matt took it off. "You don't know where it's been."

"Yes, I do," Matt contradicted, wide-eyed. "Jendra says it's been in the toilet."

Leah shuddered. She looked really grossed out. Almost too grossed out to eat. When Leah starts feeling disgusted, she literally cannot eat. As it is, she only eats enough to keep a goldfish alive! At my last birthday party—and I swear to you this is true—Leah whined about eating ice cream. She said it would make her fat. So, instead, she just ate a big bowl of ice.

Leah stared at the shoe. "Don't you wonder how it got in the toilet?" she demanded.

"It wasn't like it was *spawned* there or something," I said, rolling my eyes. "It fell off some guy's foot."

Leah cocked an eyebrow again. She does that a lot. "Some guy who just happened to be hanging out in the girls' bathroom?"

"No," I said, rolling my eyes.

Hearing that, Leah guessed darkly, "The *boys'* bathroom?" as if I had sunk to some new low.

"No," I said again. "I was in the *girls'* bathroom. And he wasn't just hanging out in there. Actually, he was hanging right above my head. Somebody was pulling his body up through a hole in the ceiling."

Leah and Matt did not look impressed.

"Don't you think that's kind of weird?" I asked desperately.

"I think *you're* kind of weird," Matt offered, "but we already knew that."

"I think somebody must be up to something sinister," I declared. "Maybe somebody murdered this man, and then dragged him up into the ceiling to hide the body."

"I'll bet that's it," Leah said sarcastically, picking the pepperoni off her pizza. She always gets the pepperoni pizza, and then she always picks the pepperoni off. I don't know why she does that! (Maybe because of that rumor somebody spread that the plain cheese pizza is made with goat's milk. Leah will believe anything—unless she hears it from me, of course.)

"You guys don't believe me, do you?" I asked suspiciously. I don't know why they never believe me!

Well, actually, I do know why. It's because I make up stuff all the time and try to convince them it's true. Like, one time I told them that our PE substitute was an Iraqi spy, and another time I told them I had a twin sister named Claudette, who for some reason lived in France (probably because she liked the croissants there so much). It's not that I want to tell lies, but, honestly, our life is so boring! I think it would be a crime not to spice it up a little when I can! Besides, sometimes I think that if I make enough people believe something is true, it will become true.

Okay! Okay! So I'm a pathological liar! So kill me!

Leah sighed and batted her eyelashes. With Leah, that's like a signal. It usually means she's about to have a fit. "I think Mr. Talbert wears loafers like that," she offered blandly. I could tell she was just humoring me. "But I'm pretty positive he's still alive, Jen. I'm sure somebody would have noticed by now if the principal had been murdered and hidden away in a girls' bathroom ceiling."

"Well, look what I found stuck to the bottom of the shoe," I said. I reached into my pocket and pulled out the piece of pompon strand. "I think there's only one possible explanation here."

"Oh, my gosh!" Matt exclaimed suddenly. He let his green eyes get really, really big before he gasped, "Mr. Talbert is really a cheerleader! No wonder he decided to make pep rallies mandatory."

I groaned at him and snatched back the shoe. "Oh, will you shut up! I'm really serious!"

"You don't think a cheerleader *killed him,* do you, Jendra?" Leah asked flatly. She was giving me one of her *Oh-you're-being-so-immature-and-just-for-that-I'm-about-to-throw-a-whiny-fit* looks.

I shrugged. "Maybe a cheerleader witnessed his . . . *abduction.*"

That shut her up pretty fast. Just hearing the word *abduction* made her tremble.

"Look, Jendra," Matt told me, "if you're wondering about the cheerleaders, why don't you just talk to Tina? I'm sure she'll be happy to answer any of your weird questions, as long as you don't take up more than five minutes of her busy schedule."

Tina Sheperd is this gorgeous, popular, smart eighth-grade cheerleader. She's the one who organizes all the cheerleading functions and makes up all the cheers. And, in her spare time, she's also Matt's cousin.

Tina always makes a really big deal about being nice and talking to everybody—the really, really popular people *and* the rest of us poor slobs, too. But, actually, it's kind of tricky to spend any kind of quality time with her unless you're somebody she considers important . . . or unless you're Matt and can blackmail her by threatening to tell her parents about the time she skipped computer science and hung out in the parking lot behind the school . . . or unless you're me, and you happen to annoy Matt until he uses his influence to force Tina to talk to you.

Actually, I had only talked to Tina once before. I was at Matt's house, sprawled out across the couch, playing video games while Matt was upstairs in the shower. And then Tina walked in and said, "Hey, Jendra."

"Hi, Tina," I replied shakily.

She smiled. "You're surprised I know your name, huh?" She had perfect teeth. White, straight, clean. Everything mine aren't.

"Yeah, kind of," I admitted.

Tina laughed warmly and said, "I know all of Mattie's friends." Then, somehow, I ended up lending her ten dollars, and she left to go to the movies with some tennis player named Jonathan. To date, that had been my only experience with Tina Sheperd.

But when Matt suggested it, I suddenly decided that asking Tina about the shoe was an excellent idea. I needed to talk to a cheerleader, after all. And if she was anything, Tina was a cheerleader. In fact, she was *the* cheerleader.

So, while Leah finished eating her picked-apart pizza, Matt led me over to the table by the window where Tina and her friends always eat lunch.

Tina looked up almost right away and saw us standing behind her. "Hi, Mattie," she said with a smile that looked sincere enough. "Hi, Jendra. Do you guys know Jamey, LaKaisha, Martin, Lisa, Andrew, Kevin, Tony, Ryan, and Keith?"

"Of course not," Matt said bluntly. "I only know *you* because your mom is my father's sister. But Jendra needs to ask you a question."

Tina raised her eyebrows, interested. "Yeah?" she said, smiling at me. She nodded at the girl sitting next to her, who immediately grabbed an empty chair from another table and slid it over next to Tina. Patting the chair, Tina told me, "Sit down. What's up?"

"Right now," I replied, "I really don't know what's up. But a few minutes ago, when I was in the bathroom, some guys' legs were dangling up above my head." I chose that moment to place the loafer on the table. Then I finished the story.

Tina took the piece of pompon from me and stared at it intently. "Bizarre!" she said, like she really meant it. At least somebody was interested in what I had to say! Slipping the piece of pompon into her pocket and taking the shoe, she said, "Well, I don't know, Jendra. I wish I had something to say. That really is strange!" She took a sip of her imported mineral water before saying, "Thanks for brightening up our lunch, anyway." She started laughing, and the rest of the table quickly joined in. "Yeah, this will give us something to talk about for a while."

13

I smiled weakly. Matt was already standing, so I slowly rose to join him.

"Oh, and Jendra," Tina added softly, her gray eyes sparkling.

"Yeah?"

"As soon as I hear anything, I promise you'll be the first to know."

I nodded. "Thanks," I told her. The bell rang and I hurried off to history.

3
The Coyote in Khakis

When that shady-looking office aide slipped me a carefully folded note, I didn't read it at first. I was too busy giving an oral report on the Battle of San Jacinto, and a very interesting oral report, too, if you ask me.

You know how some subjects just really spark your interest and make you curious to learn more? Well, since the beginning of seventh grade, I've just been dying to know one thing about Texas history.

Why we have to take it.

(You may have guessed by now that I'm not exactly preparing for a brilliant future at an Ivy League university. My dad always says that with my grades, I'll be lucky if I make it into a *Poison* Ivy League!)

Okay, so Texas history ranks right up there with math on my list of least favorite subjects. But even though I absolutely hate that class, I always do my best to make my oral reports entertaining *and* informative.

In fact, that day I'm pretty sure I said some stuff that even my teacher, Ms. Long, had never heard before.

Well, actually, I'm *positive* she hadn't heard it before because I made it all up as I went along.

"And so," I finished with flair, "Sam Houston and his men could never have won the battle of San Jacinto without the help of the courageous, unappreciated"—and made-up—"soldier Colonel Franklin S. Fillmore."

The class burst into applause. (Okay, so that might be a bit of an exaggeration. But the people who were still awake sort of clapped. When you've got your sights set on being the next Drew Barrymore, you've got to learn to overlook getting snubbed by unrefined audiences.)

As the next presenter stepped up, I returned to my seat in the back row, across the aisle from Matt.

"Way to go, Jendra," he whispered with a grin. "That was the best report since Christopher Columbus discovered *Antarctica.*"

"How would you know?" I said with a smile. "You weren't even alive back in 1942."

But then I noticed that Ms. Long was glaring at me, so I decided to shut up and read my note.

I unfolded it slowly.

In pink ink someone had written in big, round letters:

Jendra—just wanted you to be the first to know—some maniac stole Mr. Talbert's shoes

and his pants! **You'll be hearing all the details in just a few minutes. Thanks for the tip.**

It wasn't signed, but I knew it was from Tina.

Sure enough, seconds later the TV monitor mounted above the board flashed on, interrupting our class.

I don't know if your school is still back in the Dark Ages or what, but at my school, we do announcements over the closed-circuit TV system. Like Mr. Talbert told our parents, a dual-media approach gives us far more advantages than we had last year, when they just did announcements over the PA system. Now, instead of just *not listening* to the announcements, we can *not watch* them, too. That way we can ignore twice as much information! And in this crowded, crazy, multimedia world of ours, learning to ignore annoying stuff is a very useful life skill.

I don't mean to be rude, but really now, school announcements are not exactly four-star entertainment, are they? I mean, who really cares who won the district spelling bee? That's boring, B-O-R-R-I-N-G, boring. (And like you probably guessed, it wasn't me.)

That day, though, when the TV screen flashed on, everybody paid attention. Of course, anything was better than listening to those awful Texas history reports, but in addition to that, we were all really shocked.

Mr. Talbert, the principal, was standing and holding a science fair display board that covered him from the waist down. At the bottom of the board, we could see his bare feet sticking out.

At first he didn't say anything. I think that was to make sure everybody had enough time to wonder what on earth he was doing.

Then, in an extremely serious, loud voice, he announced, "Somebody stole my pants."

Our entire class burst out laughing—even Ms. Long. She stopped pretty fast, though, and looked embarrassed.

Mr. Talbert is a really cool principal. A lot of people think he's a big dork. He is, of course, but that's exactly what makes him so cool. He acts like a dork on purpose because that way he can interact with us kids better. I mean, everybody would be scared of him if he acted like some psycho Nazi prison guard all the time. This way people at least talk to him, even if they *do* roll their eyes and start laughing as soon as he turns his back. It's actually a very clever ruse. (A *ruse,* by the way, is like a trick. I learned that helping my mom grade her vocabulary tests. I pick up a lot of *efficacious* words that way.)

But I *digress* (see what I mean?). Standing there with no pants on was exactly the kind of thing Mr. Talbert would do, but he had never done it *before,* so we were all surprised.

He gave us a minute to react, and then he continued, "This morning I was sitting in my office, savoring the mountain-grown aroma of my coffee, when suddenly I looked up and saw someone sinister standing in front of me."

Pausing a moment, he continued, "He . . . *or she* . . . was wearing the costume of our beloved school mascot, the Davy Crockett Coyote, and pointing a gun directly at my head."

We didn't really know how to react to that. I

mean, should we laugh or gasp in horror? We didn't have much practice in actually *watching* the announcements, so we were really confused.

Mr. Talbert continued, "Then, the costumed criminal handed me a note, instructing me to take off my shoes, my socks, and my pants, and hand them over to him . . . *or her*. Since I feared for my life, I had no choice but to obey the outrageous demand. Once my attacker had my pants, my shoes, and my favorite pair of argyle socks, he . . . *or she* . . . dropped the gun and ran out of my office, leaving me in this"—he nodded down at the display board—"very embarrassing condition."

Suddenly he dropped the display board, and we all gasped out loud. Quite a few people actually hid their eyes, until he said, "Fortunately, I was able to use my office phone to call my devoted wife, Gloria, who quickly came to the rescue and brought me another pair of pants." He had been wearing pants the whole time, of course. The thing with the science display board was just a ploy to get our attention. (And if you're wondering, a *ploy* is just about the same thing as a *ruse*. That ol' Mr. Talbert's a pretty tricky guy.)

"What a dork!" Matt said.

"Quiet, Matthew," Ms. Long snapped. She hates it when people talk. I'll bet she never even taught her own kids *how* to talk. (She also hates Matt. And she hates me, too. For some reason, she has this idea that I'm always secretly chewing gum in her class. Like I would do that! I mean, totally lying about history is one thing, but chewing gum in class? That's breaking one of the Eleven Commandments—as anyone who heard my history report on world religions last year could tell you.)

"Thanks to the efforts of Tina Sheperd, our head cheerleader," Mr. Talbert continued, "I have recovered the bottom half of my outfit. We discovered the Crockett Coyote costume, with my pants, socks, and shoes attached, stuffed into the crawl space in the ceiling of the second-story girls' bathroom. Pinned to the costume's furry chest was a piece of crumpled notebook paper containing a very insulting and unrepeatable remark about the cheerleaders. The culprit, I regret to inform you, is still at large."

Mr. Talbert strolled over to the door of his office, and the camera followed him. He knelt down and picked up a gun. Then he pointed it at the camera, and gently pulled the trigger, firing a tiny stream of water.

"Because an actual firearm was not used," he said, "I am willing to overlook the assault on my person and not press criminal charges. But we cannot have our school overrun by foul-mouthed coyote kidnappers who have no respect for the position of the cheerleaders or the pants of the principal. If you know who committed this heinous heist, please come down to the principal's office right away to file your anonymous report. You will be generously rewarded. Thank you. Teachers, pardon this interruption, you may now return to your regularly scheduled classroom activities. But, remember—never take your pants for granted. Bye now!" Mr. Talbert waved cheerfully, and the TV turned itself off.

"How psycho!" Matt said loudly. "I wonder what the reward is?"

Ms. Long glared at him. Then, just because she hates me so much, I guess, she glared at me, too.

I figured since she was already glaring at me, it couldn't hurt to answer Matt. "Probably more of those leftover free passes to Bowl-a-Rama," I told him knowingly. I swear, Bowl-a-Rama must not have *any* customers, because they're always trying to give away free passes to kids at my school, and nobody will ever take them.

"Crime is not a thing to joke about, Ms. MacKenzie," Ms. Long said sternly, glaring even harder. She stared at me for a really long time. Maybe she thought I was chewing gum again. Or maybe she was thinking of turning me in to Mr. Talbert for some free bowling passes. Now that I think about it, Ms. Long seems exactly like the type who would enjoy a visit to Bowl-a-Rama. Nobody ever goes there, so it's probably nice and quiet all the time. Right up her alley! (That's a pun. Get it? My mom thinks William Shakespeare's puns are brilliant, but when her students use puns in essays, she usually takes off like twenty points. I'm not looking forward to high school.)

Just then—the timing couldn't have been more perfect—some kid with a laminated badge came to the door and said I was supposed to go to the principal's office.

Ms. Long smiled at me smugly. I'm sure she thought I was the one behind the whole coyote incident. "You'd better run along," she advised with an evil grin, looking not unlike a coyote herself. (She does have kind of a long, pointy nose, as a matter of fact. Maybe she really is a coyote—one who discovered Mary Kay cosmetics and then managed to get a teaching certificate.)

As I walked out of the room with the office aide,

Matt called after me, "Be sure you spit out your gum first, Jendra!" He's such a jerk.

Looking over my shoulder, I saw Matt laughing, and Ms. Long glaring away.

Why on earth did they want me in the principal's office? I had no idea.

4
A Strange Reward

Actually, that's a total lie. I had a very good idea why they wanted me in the principal's office. In fact, I was almost positive it had something to do with the shoe.

I was right.

When I walked into the office, Mr. Talbert was sitting behind his desk, grinning at me.

"Well, Jendra, you really saved the day." I thought Mr. Talbert's voice had gotten awfully high, and airy, and female sounding until I spotted Tina standing over in the corner. She was the one who had spoken and was now grinning at me.

I shrugged. "You mean because I found Mr. Talbert's shoe? That was no big deal."

"Oh yes it was," Mr. Talbert assured me. "I've got plenty of spare pants, but that was my only pair of

23

loafers." He waved for me to move closer. "I think you deserve a reward." He reached into the pocket of his suit and handed me a sealed white envelope. "Can you guess what's in there?"

"Nooo," I lied sweetly. I could see he wanted to surprise me, and I couldn't disappoint him. The whole time, I was thinking *Bowl-a-Rama, Bowl-a-Rama, Bowl-a-Rama....*

But when I opened up the envelope, the only thing inside was a little slip of paper with a bunch of numbers written on it. 24-19-32

At first I thought it was a date, but then I realized that wouldn't exactly work. I mean, what could the 24 possibly stand for—December times two?

"Surprised?" Mr. Talbert asked me.

"Oh, yes," I said honestly. I stared at the paper again. Before I thought about it, I wrinkled up my nose and raised one eyebrow. Then I thought that probably looked stupid, so I said very politely, "Yes, sir. I couldn't be more surprised."

"It was Tina's idea," Mr. Talbert said.

I stared at the numbers. Then I stared over at Tina. "Good idea," I said finally. I didn't know what else to say. What do you say when somebody gives you a bunch of numbers?

Tina laughed. It was a strange laugh. I couldn't tell if she was being friendly or if she thought I was a stupid little moron.

"It's a locker combination, Jendra," she said. "We're making you a cheerleader."

I almost died. *"What?"* I blurted out in shock.

Tina laughed again, a light, airy little laugh. "Well, you *are* surprised, aren't you?" she said.

I bit my lip. "Are you kidding?" I asked flatly. I

sort of hoped she was. I figured if she'd ever seen me try to do aerobics, she had to be kidding. Let's put it this way. The cerebellum is the part of your brain that controls balance and graceful, coordinated movements. I don't think I have one. In fact, I know I don't.

"She's completely serious," Mr. Talbert said with a smile. "Aren't you excited?"

"Well, I'm . . ."—*really confused*—"flattered," I said carefully. "But I didn't know you could just make somebody a cheerleader like that—especially in the middle of the year."

"You can't," said Tina, "but I can. After all, didn't you hear Mr. Talbert? I just did." She smiled serenely and took my hand. "Let me show you the way to the locker room."

I already knew the way to the locker room, and I didn't want to go. But I didn't want to be rude, either. So, I said good-bye to Mr. Talbert and followed Tina out into the hall.

"I can't dance," I told her frankly. "And I can't do gymnastics, either. Last year during our gymnastics unit, when I tried to do a handstand up against the wall, I kicked the girl next to me in the head, and she had to go to the nurse." (That was Leah, by the way, and she whined about it for the rest of the week.)

Tina watched me closely while I talked. Her gray eyes were twinkling as they stared right into mine. "That doesn't matter," she assured me. "I like your school spirit."

"You do?" I squeaked. I didn't know I had any school spirit.

"Of course," she said. "You defended our honor.

25

You stood up for the cheerleaders. You showed your loyalty to Crockett."

"All I was trying to do was skip the last half of algebra," I admitted.

"Another thing to recommend you," Tina said with a smile. She tossed her hair. "Honestly, Jendra, have you ever known any cheerleader to sit through an entire algebra class?"

"I don't know," I answered honestly. "You're the only cheerleader I've ever known."

We had reached the locker room by then, and I was starting to feel really uncomfortable. I'll be honest. With *my* background, and my underwhelming level of popularity, beauty, and grace, I had never even thought about being a cheerleader. And I just didn't feel like I fit the profile. I mean, I'm pretty average looking and a lot of those girls are *really beautiful*.

"You know, Jendra," Tina said suddenly, "you are *really beautiful*." That was weird! It was like she was reading my mind or something.

I must have looked shocked because she said, "Don't be embarrassed. I know you were just thinking the same thing about me. But it's true. You've got such a pretty face. It's a shame no one will be able to see it."

"What do you mean?" I asked. For a minute I was kind of scared my life was going to turn into some kind of horror movie. You know, *Terror in the Locker Room*? Like Tina was going to whip out a meat cleaver and slice off my face or something. Well, okay, so I wasn't *really* scared. I was actually sort of enjoying the idea. (I like to keep myself entertained with stupid little fantasies like that.) But if I would have known then what I know now! I mean, I never even . . .

Well, anyway . . .

"What do you mean nobody will be able to see my face?" I asked.

She smiled and explained, "I'm going to make you the mascot." She led me over to my locker. "So, you see, it won't make a difference if you can't dance or flip or"—her gray eyes lit up as she smiled almost imperceptibly—"anything. So, will I see you at practice this afternoon?"

She was being really nice to me, of course. And her voice was very soft and sweet. But I kind of got the feeling that she wasn't going to take no for an answer.

I gave it one last try. "I don't think I'll be able to go to the games," I said. "I'm practically failing pre-algebra."

"I'm sure your grades will be better by Friday night," Tina said.

"I don't think I can pull them up by then," I told her.

"Oh, you can't," Tina agreed, moving toward the door. She added with a wink. "But I can."

She walked out of the locker room and flicked off the lights. As I stood there in the dark, I heard her call over her shoulder, "See you at practice this afternoon."

5
The Old Mascot

"You have to go to cheerleading practice?!" Leah repeated in a shrill whine. I could see she didn't believe me. We were standing in front of the library after school, and I was trying to explain to her why I couldn't go to the movies with her that afternoon.

"I know it sounds weird—" I began.

"Weird?" Leah exclaimed. "No joke!" She started blinking and batting her eyelashes really fast like she does when she's upset. I always worry that her eyelashes are going to get stuck together because Leah wears more mascara than anybody I know. The way she globs it on, it's gotta be pretty sticky. Actually, it looks like tar.

"It'll only be for a couple of hours," I promised. "There's really no way I can get out of it. We could always go after practice."

"Some of us," Leah informed me with another few flutters, "actually *do* homework."

I was going to point out to her that going to the movies takes the same amount of time no matter what time of the day you do it, but I got sort of hypnotized watching her eyelash action. Probably just as well that I didn't say anything. She was already about to have a stroke right there at the top of the stairs.

"Just because you found that stupid shoe!" Leah yelled. "Mr. Talbert explained all about that on TV. It was just a stupid prank! You don't have to stalk the cheerleaders!"

I rolled my eyes. "I am *not*," I said, "stalking the cheerleaders. You never listen, Leah. I told you, Tina asked me to be a cheerleader. But maybe my voice was drowned out by your eyelashes fluttering."

"Tina wants *you* to be a *cheerleader?*" Leah repeated.

I nodded and then added, "Well, actually, the mascot. She figures that since I found the shoe and all, I can probably help her find out who was behind the whole thing. And she said the mascot costume would be a good disguise for me." Tina had never said anything even remotely like that, but it sounded like a good idea to me, and I could see that Leah needed an explanation.

Apparently, though, my explanation wasn't good enough. Leah cocked an eyebrow at me. "What happened to the *old* mascot?" she asked.

Actually, that was a pretty good question. I had never thought about it myself. But suddenly I wanted to know that, too. With a sigh I tried to sound annoyed as I said quickly, "She moved to Finland."

"You're lying," Leah said.

I tried to look offended. "Oh, come on, Leah. Don't you think I could come up with a better lie than that? *She moved to Finland.* Does that sound like a typical lie to you?" She was right, of course. I *was* lying. But if I would have told her the truth, that I had absolutely *no clue* what happened to the other mascot, she would have jumped on that and thrown an even bigger fit.

"Jendra MacKenzie, this is completely ridiculous," Leah informed me. She was far from calm. "This is the most ridiculous thing you've done in at least three weeks. And I just want you to know, for the record, that I think you're being ridiculous. You ought to know that you can't trust Tina Sheperd."

"Why not?" I demanded.

"Because," Leah said, batting her eyelashes at me, "she's *Tina Sheperd.* And in middle school you can't trust anybody who the entire student body knows by reputation." Leah comes up with these little pearls of wisdom all the time. It's really very annoying. "Besides," she added, "you know all the stuff Matt's said about her. She's selfish and shallow and self-absorbed, and she's used to getting her own way. She doesn't care about other people at all. She's completely insensitive."

I groaned. "Leah, she didn't ask me to marry her," I said with a sigh. "She just wants me to come to cheerleading practice a couple times and be the stupid mascot. Besides, you can't go by what Matt says. He's her cousin. I mean, you always say that your cousin in high school is a spoiled brat, too."

"She *is,*" Leah said seriously. "And Tina is, too." She sighed heavily and turned her back on me.

"Call me when you get home and tell me how practice went," she said, like she had given up on me. "But I can't promise I'll have time to talk to you. I might be too busy doing my homework."

I rolled my eyes as Leah disappeared down the stairs.

On the way back to the locker room, I ran into Tina, who I guess was coming to get me. She had already changed into her cheerleading uniform and was now lugging around a science display board. It looked like the same one Mr. Talbert had used on TV.

"Hey, Jendra," she said with a slight toss of her hair. "You are coming to practice—right?"

"Yeah," I said, feeling almost guilty. Like she had caught me in a lie. That was weird because I really *had* been on my way to practice. But Tina made me kind of nervous.

"Great," she said with a smile. "I was just running down to the science room to return this display board to Dr. Murphy. Why don't you come with me?"

"Okay," I said, falling into step behind her.

Dr. Murphy is the physical science teacher at our school. He teaches over at the high school in the mornings because not very many people get to take physical science in eighth grade—only the really smart ones. Like Tina. Not only is she taking physical science, she also helps Dr. Murphy tutor people after school. Matt told me about it. He told me Tina's *really* smart, and that she *really* knows it, too.

He also told me some *really* weird stuff about Dr. Murphy. Not that I believe it, or anything. I mean, the way Matt tells it, Columbus sailed on the *Niña,* the *Pinta,* and the *Piña Colada,* so Matt's not exactly the most reliable source in the world.

Still, his stories make interesting enough lunch fare.

Like the one about how even though Dr. Murphy is a double Ph.D., he has to teach junior high kids now because he got fired from some big deal, high-profile research laboratory out in San Francisco. Evidently he was doing unauthorized experiments after hours.

Ever since I heard that, I've sort of wondered what kind of experiments you would have to do to get fired from a research laboratory. I mean, eat one amoeba and you lose lab privileges in our class, but at an actual research laboratory, you'd think they'd be a little more open-minded. (And, in my opinion, if you've gone to all the trouble of getting a double Ph.D., you should be allowed to eat as many amoebas as you want—for whatever that's worth.)

Matt's best guess was that the whole scandal centered around human cloning. He and I spent many a dreary history slide show passing cloning notes back and forth—until Leah spoiled all our fun by informing us that some labs are actually doing that. Then, for a long time I toyed with the idea that Dr. Murphy had been filling up the Erlenmeyer flasks with multicolored sand and making a little extra cash on the side. Seemed funny at the time. Oh, man! If I had ever once suspected what kind of freaky stuff Dr. Murphy did in that laboratory, I . . .

Well, it's too soon to get into all of that now. But I sure wouldn't have been following Tina down the hall to the science room! As it was I was a little anxious. Leah had scared me just a bit.

"Tina," I asked slowly—I wasn't sure if I should ask her or not, it made me kind of nervous—"what happened to the girl who used to be the mascot?"

"Chrystal?" Tina said lightly. She lowered her voice and told me in a whisper, "Don't talk about it, okay? But she told me yesterday that she wanted to quit. I was trying to talk her out of it, but then Mr. Talbert and I found that note." She shuddered.

"The note that was pinned to the mascot?" I said. I didn't understand.

"I know you don't understand," Tina told me calmly. It was absolutely creepy the way she did that! "But it's not something I want to talk about right here in the hall. I'll explain later if I get the chance. Don't mention it to the girls at practice," she added with a secretive look in her gray eyes. "They're scared enough as it is."

Now I was really curious. I was still thinking about it when we got to Dr. Murphy's room. Of course, that wasn't such a big surprise since it took us about two minutes to get there. But for me, keeping my mind on the same subject for two minutes is quite an accomplishment.

The light in the physical science room was on, but nobody answered when we knocked on the door. The room wasn't locked, though.

"Dr. Murphy?" Tina called, poking her head inside. "Dr. Murphy? Stephen?"

"Stephen?" I repeated.

"He's a friend of the family," Tina explained, peering inside the room and calling his name again. There was no answer.

"He must have gone out for a minute," Tina decided. She opened the door and stepped into the classroom.

I wasn't sure if I should follow her. "Can we go into a classroom when the teacher's not there?" I asked.

Tina laughed a little and said, "I can."

So I followed her in.

"He'll probably be back in a minute or two," Tina told me, glancing down at her watch, "but we have to get to practice. We don't have time to wait. I'll just drop off the board. Wait here a minute, Jendra."

I didn't have much choice. She took the board and disappeared into the storage room in the back. After a few seconds of twiddling my thumbs, I tiptoed toward the back of the room, too. Like I said, I have a short attention span, and I couldn't help being curious.

Peering through the storage-room window, I noticed an awful lot of boxes back there. (Multicolored sand maybe? Human clones perhaps?) One of the boxes stood out from the others. It was black, and labeled "Forbidden Box—Evil Chemical Solution Inside." Well, actually, I may be making that up from later memories, but it said something like that. The box was open, and Tina was leaning over it, but before I could see what was inside, she whirled around and stared straight into my eyes.

"Jendra," she said. I jumped. "I told you to wait." She flung open the door imperiously and shut it quickly behind her. "Now get back to the front of the classroom."

"Sorry," I mumbled. "I just . . . uhm . . . I . . ."

Just then Dr. Murphy came into the room holding a stack of Scantron forms. "Hello, Tina," he said when he saw us there.

She smiled at him. "This is Jendra MacKenzie, Dr. Murphy," she said. "She's going to be our new mascot."

Dr. Murphy frowned and said, "Has she heard about the—"

Tina quickly waved a hand in the air, which shut him up almost immediately. "There are a few things I still have to tell her," she said quietly. Then, turning to me, she said, "Come on, Jendra, we should get to the gym."

6

Some Threats, a Scar, and a Rabid Coyote

*T*he color brown has never really done much for me, and in the coyote costume I looked disturbingly rabid even without the mask on. "Are you sure you *really* want *me* to do this?" I squeaked, turning to Tina.

"You're the *only* one I'd even consider," she said, leading me out of the locker room. That kind of surprised me. But I figured that she was just being nice.

On the far side of the gym a bunch of tall, sweaty seventh- and eighth-grade guys—including Matt—were playing basketball. Three or four cheerleaders were over there, too, flirting with the guys, I guess. But the rest of them were over on the other side of the room, stuffing little party-favor-type things into white lunch sacks that were sitting in a row on a long wooden bench.

Just as Tina and I stepped out of the locker room, the basketball coach also appeared. The boys instantly focused on their game, and the stray cheerleaders scampered back over to our side.

"Who's *she?*" one of them chirped. She sounded friendly enough, but she was staring at me kind of suspiciously.

"Jendra MacKenzie, *of course,*" Tina told her airily with a slight toss of her hair and an incredulous look in her gray eyes. I wondered why she had added that "of course" that way. I mean, these were some of the most popular girls in the school. It wasn't like any of them should have heard of someone like me.

But I guess I was wrong because as soon as Tina said my name, the rest of them all started saying things like, "Oh, Jendra MacKenzie!"

"Jendra MacKenzie!"

"This is Jendra?"

"Oh, okay. It's Jendra!"

I smiled at them uneasily. I wanted to put on my coyote head and disappear for a while, but from the way Tina was looking at me, I got the impression that wasn't an option.

"We've been dying to meet you, Jendra," said a girl with raven black hair streaked with red. She widened her gray eyes and added, "I'm surprised you're not a cheerleader already. I mean, you *are* really beautiful." The rest of the girls nodded vigorously, all smiling at me in kind of a weird way.

I was starting to feel very self-conscious. "Well,

I've never been much of an athlete. . . ." I fumbled nervously.

Fortunately, Tina took charge of the conversation. "Jendra," she said in that Tina voice of hers, with one of those self-confident Tina smiles, "right now we're all stuffing goodie bags for the basketball boys. You know, as sort of an incentive for victory Friday night. So you don't have to worry about anything athletic just yet. Come on now, why don't you lend a hand?"

I smiled shakily and tried to pick up a sack, using both paws.

The cheerleaders all laughed at me. "Those paws are fastened on with Velcro," the girl with the red-streaked black hair told me. "You might have more luck if you take them off. By the way, I'm Lien Hua. Lien Hua Le."

"And I'm Jamey Fitzhughston," said a tiny blond girl with enormous gray eyes. Actually, she was the one who had stared suspiciously at me earlier, and she still didn't seem to like me very much. "This is Deidre, and that's Vanessa, and this is Amber, and that's LaKaisha, and that's Jennifer Rosmand and Jennifer Martinez, and Kyla, and Erica, and Mitzi and Leigh."

All the cheerleaders smiled real big for like three seconds when Jamey called their names, and right after that, they let their faces go back to normal again. Except Lien Hua.

Lien Hua kept smiling at me as she ran her fingers through her short black hair. "Grab a Twinkie," she said with a wink, grabbing my right paw and yanking it off.

Hesitantly I ripped the other paw off, and then I picked up a Twinkie and started to unwrap it.

"Don't eat it!" Tina cried in horror, pulling my hand away from my mouth and practically ripping my arm off. She threw the Twinkie across the gym and almost made a basket.

"Hey!" I said as I winced in pain. "My *arm's* not attached with Velcro, you know."

"I'm sorry," Tina said with a soothing smile. I couldn't tell if she was really sorry or not. "I didn't mean to snap at you like that. But now, honestly, Jendra, you must realize that Twinkies are extremely fattening. Don't take this the wrong way, but our mascot's supposed to be a *coyote,* not a *cow."*

The other cheerleaders laughed mischievously. Personally, I felt a little strange. Not that Tina hurt my feelings or anything. I mean I'm *not* fat. I only weigh about 114 pounds. Could be worse—you know?

But it sort of bothered me, the way Tina had seemed so horrified by the thought of me eating a Twinkie. I mean, she didn't even wait for it to get near my lips. The instant I started unwrapping it, she just threw it across the room. Now, I've heard of being health conscious, but I mean, *really.*

I must have had a funny look on my face because Tina smiled at me and reached into her purse, which was underneath the bench. She pulled out a pack of cinnamon gum and handed me a piece. "Here," she said, slipping it between my fingers. "Try this instead. Gum has practically no calories." She smiled.

I started chewing the gum and then everybody went back to stuffing the sacks full of snack food and tacky little prizes—like plastic tops, and scratch-'n'-sniff stickers, and stuff. Except for me,

everybody was chattering away while they worked.
I'd write down what they said, but it wasn't really
anything too important. And besides, I couldn't
repeat about ninety-five percent of the words they
used in print, anyway. I only said a few things
myself, mainly when they asked me direct questions.

Jamey Fitzhughston kept staring at me with
those huge gray eyes of hers the entire time. "So,
how do you like being a cheerleader and listening in
on our private conversations?" she finally asked.
"Must make you feel pretty important, huh?"
(Actually, that's not *exactly* what she said. I had to
leave out about eighteen words, just in case my
mom ever reads this.)

"I guess," I replied lamely.

Lien Hua started giggling. She turned to me and
said, "You don't cuss, do you?"

That sounded kind of funny to me, the way she
said it. It reminded me of this stupid old movie I
saw once, where this snotty guy and his snotty girl-
friend are playing tennis at the country club, and
he turns to this other guy who's just sort of standing there and says, "You don't play, do you?"

I mean, cussing has its place, I guess, but I don't
really think of it as a competitive sport.

Evidently Jamey did, though, and I kind of think
she was going for the gold, if you know what I
mean. The only one of them who didn't really have
a dirty mouth was Tina. In fact, I don't think I
heard one particle of profanity pass her lips.

Jamey was glaring at Tina, too. Finally she said,
"You showed it to her, didn't you?" (That's the cen-
sored version, of course.) Jamey sounded really cold

and angry, which is the worst kind of angry there is, in my opinion.

"Showed me what?" I squeaked.

"My appendicitis scar," Tina told me quickly. "I like to show it to everybody. See?" And with that, she bent down the top half of her skirt—right there in the gym. About that time a lot of commotion came from the boys' side, and all the guys started falling all over one another. As a reflex, I turned to look at them and saw that they were looking over at us, specifically at Tina. When I turned back, I noticed Tina glaring pointedly at Jamey.

"Listen," I said. I had the feeling that I was causing conflict. "I really don't think this is going to work out for me. I mean, if I'm a cheerleader, I'll have to go to the basketball game Friday night, and I know my algebra teacher will never—"

"Oh, Jendra, that reminds me," Tina said smoothly. "I have a few little tricks to teach you about how to handle teachers. The first step toward good grades is a good relationship." She smiled angelically and handed me the goodie bag she had just finished filling. "Why don't you take one of these to your pre-algebra teacher?"

"Okay," I said shakily, taking the bag from her. Believe me, I was pretty glad to have any excuse to get out of there.

"Lien Hua can go with you," Tina suggested. She stared at her, long and hard, and said, *"Right,* Lien Hua?"

"Sure," chirped Lien Hua with a smile. She always seemed to smile. I wondered if she ever frowned.

Lien Hua and I started out of the gym. When we

were in the middle of the hall, she pulled me aside, over by the water fountain, for a talk.

"We didn't want to scare you, Jendra," she said. "But if you're going to stay on the squad, there are a few things you need to know."

"Actually," I said weakly, "I've been meaning to talk to someone about that. I'm not so sure I want to stay on the squad at all, and I . . ."

Lien Hua wasn't even listening to me. She was busy digging around in her chain-mail purse. "Here," she said, pulling out a big wad of paper. "I think you should take a look at this." Her tone sounded really ominous, but when I looked at her face, I saw that she was still smiling. I guess she just smiled all the time.

She put the wad of paper into my palm.

"Every paper in there is a threatening note to Chrystal. Look!"

She unwrapped one sheet and showed it to me. Ever seen one of those creepy ransom notes in the movies, made out of cut-up newspaper headlines? That's exactly what she showed me. It looked really weird, and it said:

**BeWARe ChRYStal,
SOmeBoDy PoISoned YoUR POmPOnS!**

"What does that mean?" I asked.

Lien Hua shrugged. "Creepy, though, right?" she said solemnly, still smiling. "Chrystal kept finding one of those stuck in her cheerleading locker every single day for weeks. Finally she got scared, and yesterday she quit. We're kind of worried about her. I mean, we all really like her." She wrinkled her nose but kept smiling, as she added, "Except Jamey Fitzhughston. She doesn't like anybody."

"Gosh, " I said, "that's—"

But Lien Hua didn't let me finish. She stuffed the notes back down into her purse, grabbed me by the arm, and dragged me down the hall to the teacher's lounge.

"You can just put the goodie bag inside her box," she said with a smile. "Sign it, 'From a Secret Admirer.' Trust me. That works every time."

"Okay," I said, still feeling a little creepy. I stuffed the bag into Mrs. O'Donnahee's box, and then together we went back to the gym, where everybody else was learning a dance routine.

7
Bad News

For some reason Mrs. O'Donnahee wasn't in school the next day. When I mentioned it to Tina at lunch, she just said, "Great," and let me have one of her Jolly Ranchers.

Leah, however, was not so calm. "Jendra, something is definitely wrong," she told me, picking the cheese off her pizza.

"What are you doing?" I asked. "I thought you only picked the pepperoni off your pizza, now it's the cheese, too?"

"Cheese is so fattening," Leah said, "and it makes the pizza taste so gross."

"Yeah," I said, "but without the pepperoni and without the cheese your pizza is just warm sauce and bread. Does that really taste good to you?"

"Taste has nothing to do with it," Leah insisted.

44

"It's all about nutrition. And, besides, I can feed the cheese to Matt."

"No, thanks," groaned Matt, looking kind of green.

"Hey," I said, "what's wrong with you? Practice too hard last night?"

"I don't know," Matt wailed, throwing his head down on the table with a loud thump. "I just feel sort of queasy or something."

"See, I told you," Leah said wisely. "This cheese is poison. It's clogging his arteries right now here at lunch!"

"Oh, for heaven's sake, Leah," I groaned. "It isn't the pizza. There's something really wrong with him. Anybody can see that." Actually, I was kind of worried about Matt. His face was all sweaty and his skin felt clammy and cold.

"Maybe you should go to the nurse's office," I suggested.

"Nah," said Matt, looking really puky. "Then I'll miss Ms. Long's class, and I have to give a report on the Karankawa Indians today."

"Matt, you look like you just got *attacked* by the Karankawa Indians," I told him, feeling his forehead. "Aren't they the ones who greased themselves down with alligator fat so they wouldn't get bitten by mosquitoes? 'Cause, Matt, that's exactly what you smell like."

"Hi, Mattie sweetie, something wrong?" A breeze of Chanel No. 5 mixed with Salon Selectives shampoo blew by our table, and I looked up and saw Tina. She looked concerned. "Mattie," she said, "you're all sweaty and gross. That can't be good." She gently shoved Leah's chair over to one side, and crouched next to Matt with a sorrowful expression. "What have I told you about cafeteria food?" she said with an exaggerated sigh. "Dear boy, will you ever learn? Here." She pulled something in a glass jar out of her purse and set it on the table in front of him.

Matt cocked an eyebrow. "Baby applesauce?" he groaned.

"That's right," she said. "Now eat it all up good for Mommy and you'll feel all better in no time." She stood up, tossed her hair, and told me, "Jendra, I need to talk to you. Could you come over to my table for a minute, please?"

"Sure," I said. I followed her back to her usual seat while Leah looked after us, indignantly scooting her chair back into place.

"Now, Jendra," said Tina, once we had gotten back to her table, "I don't mean to sound like a snob, or anything, but I really don't think it's such a good idea for you to eat lunch with those two anymore."

"Why not?" I asked. "I mean, Leah is my best friend, and Matt is your own cousin."

"I know," said Tina regretfully, gray eyes wide. "I know, I know, I know. And it isn't that there's anything wrong with them, believe me. It's just that I think you should eat over here with the rest of the cheerleaders. That's only right. Don't you think so, girls?"

She let her eyes slide slyly first to one side and then the other, and before long all of her friends were nodding enthusiastically and offering me sips of diet soda and pieces of fat-free pretzels. Not exactly gourmet, but, I have to tell you, the pretzels were just a bit more appetizing than Leah's cheese-less pizza.

"I'm glad you came to eat with us," said Lien Hua, grinning at me as the lunch bell rang. "We really missed you."

"Yeah, " I said, returning her smile. "Well, I'll see you this afternoon at practice, okay?"

"Before that, I hope," said Lien Hua with a grin. I started off to class.

Just outside Ms. Long's room, Tina glided by me in the hall.

"Here," she said, tossing me a stick of gum. "Have a piece. It will keep your breath fresh for up to three hours."

"Thanks," I said shakily, popping it into my mouth as I shoved through the classroom door.

I expected Matt's oral report on the Karankawa Indians to be a total flop, but he completely fooled me. Somehow, he was like one hundred percent totally better by the time class started, and he gave his report like a pro. It was almost as good as mine, and just as made up, I assure you.

"Excellent work, Matt," I told him as he slid back into his seat.

"Yeah?" he said with a grin. "Well, I have an excellent role model!"

I smiled and was about to say something back, when Ms. Long sneaked up behind me and started screaming her head off. She really scared me. (Well, okay, maybe "screaming her head off" is a bit of an exaggeration. I just like to use hyperbole! You know, that goes with the territory when your mom's an English teacher. But, anyway, Ms. Long sure wasn't being very nice to me.)

"Miss MacKenzie," she shrieked. "Are you chewing gum?"

"No," I quipped instantly, rolling my eyes reflexively. "It just so happens that I . . ."—then I remembered the stick of gum Tina had popped into my mouth and finished lamely—"am." I smiled weakly.

Now, I'll admit, as your average, everyday suburban Texas teen, I've never looked the devil in the eye, but at that moment Ms. Long looked distinctly evil. Her lips twisted into this sinister smile, and she said almost gleefully, "Miss MacKenzie, go to the office immediately." She added menacingly, "And never come back."

"Never?" squeaked Matt. "Gosh, that's harsh for one piece of gum. Not even tomorrow?"

He shouldn't have said that. You don't crack jokes with the devil.

"For that smart remark, my funny man," Ms. Long informed him crisply, "you may go to the office with her."

"Do *I* have to come back?" he had the guts to ask.

That broke Ms. Long. Wrinkling her nose in rage, she screamed, "Get out of my classroom!"

Matt and I ran through the door and down the hall, giggling all the way.

Things didn't seem so funny once we got to the office, though.

Mr. Talbert was standing in the doorway of his office, talking in a real low voice to one of the school secretaries. We couldn't hear what they were saying, but, just from the looks on their faces, Matt and I figured that something was very wrong.

"It's Chrystal," said Tina, who was suddenly standing behind us.

"Where did you come from?" Matt asked, sounding as shocked as I felt.

"Home ec," she replied, smacking her Cinnaburst. "We were microwaving S'mores, but, of course, I dropped my marshmallows to rush right down here as soon as I heard the news."

"What news?" I asked. "Is something wrong?"

"Well, there's definitely something wrong with Chrystal," she said. "She's dead."

8
The Vanishing Chrystal

"Dead?" I repeated in horror. "Do you mean really, really, *really* dead? Really?"

"Really," said Tina.

"Really?" I guess I'm kind of a skeptic. This cynical age we live in has left its mark on me in a big way. I mean, I know it probably sounds weird that I didn't believe her at first, but keep in mind I had never personally known anyone who was really dead before—except my great-aunt, Mildred, and I didn't really *know* her. Well, technically, I didn't really *know* Chrystal either, but I knew she must have been about my size because I fit into her coyote suit.

Tina rolled her gray eyes at me and tossed her hair. "Actually, Jendra," she said with a groan, "she's not really dead. But she might as well be as far as we're concerned. I guess somebody scared her really, really a lot. So she withdrew from school and moved to Australia."

"Australia?" I repeated with a frown.

"That's the official story anyway," Tina said. The secretive look she gave me just then made me shudder. What was the *un*official story?

"I'm not so sure I can make it to practice this afternoon," I announced, looking traumatized. "I just got kicked out of history class. We're here to see Mr. Talbert."

Tina laughed. "Practice? Well, don't worry, Jendra, that's probably canceled after this mess. And don't worry about Mr. Talbert. I'll talk to him for you. Also, there's probably not going to be a game Friday night."

"What?" Matt exclaimed. "That's crazy! What do you mean? We've been practicing all week!"

Tina shrugged. "Don't yell at me," she said. "I can't help it. I don't make the rules." I wasn't so sure about that, personally. "The thing is," she went on, "and this is *really* weird—Mr. Talbert suspects that someone on the basketball team might have scared Chrystal away."

"What?" yelped Matt. "Why? That's totally crazy!"

"But totally probable," said Tina. "I guess you're the only member of the team who's still at school, Mattie. All the rest of them either didn't come in today or went home sick. Like some weird, convenient basketball flu. You've got to admit that that looks pretty sinister."

"Maybe they're just tired," Matt reasoned. "We did practice pretty hard. I mean, come on, Tina. Just because they didn't come to school, that doesn't mean they terrorized some girl. That's kind of a stretch if you ask me."

Tina shrugged again. "The basketball players are looking pretty suspicious right now," she said. "Mr. Talbert thinks they might be the ones who stole his pants and his shoes. Remember last week's school paper? The star player was quoted as saying how much he wished he had shoes like Mr. Talbert's. And the point guard commented on his pants."

I did remember those quotes. They had even made a big deal about them on the announcements. Everybody in the whole school probably remembered.

Matt rolled his eyes. "Like they really want to dress like a middle-aged **principal**!" he said, sounding exasperated. "Tina, they just said that stuff to score points with Mr. Talbert."

"Really?" she probed. "Are you sure they didn't want to score a new outfit?"

Matt rolled his eyes again.

"Well, I've got to go," Tina said lightly. "Mr. Talbert wants to talk to me right away." She grinned, looking lofty, and added, "You know, important stuff. But, Jen, don't go too far, okay? I'll have Lien Hua get in touch with you, because practice or no practice, we really need to have a meeting this afternoon to discuss all this, okay? Great to see you."

She strolled off down the hall.

"Don't go too far?" I repeated in confusion. "It's the middle of the school day, Matt! Where the heck does she think I'm going? I probably can't even get back into class."

"Tina's weird," Matt said. "I wouldn't pay too much attention to her. She's kind of stuck on her own importance. Actually, Jendra, if I were you, I would stop hanging around with her. I know it might sound crazy, but she has this way of getting people into really serious trouble. In fact, if I were you, I wouldn't trust her at all."

I probably should have listened to him, but at the time I decided he was being a jealous cousin.

"Sure, Matt," I assured him. "I'll watch out for myself. But don't worry, okay? Tina's been great. She's helping us with Mr. Talbert. In fact, she's one of the nicest people I know."

Man, I am so stupid!

9
Lien Hua

The weird thing about Lien Hua was that whenever I was with her, it was like I forgot about everything else I was supposed to be doing.

I noticed that for the first time later that afternoon. I had been talking to Lien Hua for like ten minutes in the band hall bathroom when I suddenly realized I was supposed to be in computer science. And, believe me, that's a lot to forget.

"Oh, my gosh!" I exclaimed, looking at my watch. "Great! I'm like a million years late. I'm going to be sent to the office twice in one day!"

Lien Hua didn't seem too worried. She just laughed. "Relax," she assured me. "You're not going to get in trouble. Tina will take care of it. She'll make sure your stupid computer teacher doesn't give you a tardy. What's her name?"

"*Her* name is *Mr.* Grady," I said. "But I really don't think anybody can stop him from giving me a tardy."

Lien Hua smiled. Well, actually, it wasn't like she hadn't been smiling before, so I guess I should say she continued smiling. It's just that that sounds kind of weird, you know? Oh, well. Lien Hua *continued smiling* and assured me with a wink, "Tina can." I had heard that one before.

"Tina can do anything, can't she?" I said.

"Pretty much," Lien Hua agreed with a smile.

"It's weird," I said to her. "I mean, it's like she's got some kind of magic power or something."

Lien Hua smiled. Well, okay! Okay! Lien Hua *continued smiling.* She told me, "She does."

"She does?"

Lien Hua laughed. "You'll see," she said. "Just wait until your initiation."

"Initiation?"

"This afternoon," she told me. "At Jamey Fitzhughston's house."

Oh, great, I thought. *Jamey Fitzhughston hates me. I think she'd kill me if she had half a chance.*

"Probably," Lien Hua agreed.

It took me a minute to realize that something was a little bit off in that exchange. "Hold on!" I said suddenly. "You just answered me, and I didn't say anything out loud!"

"Oh, sorry," chirped Lien Hua. She continued smiling. "I guess I do that sometimes. Déjà vu, right?"

"Déjà vu?" I repeated in confusion. "That's not what that means."

"Well, whatever!" she said, continuing to smile.

I was starting to feel kind of creeped out by then. "Listen," I said. "I really think I should be getting back to class."

Probably, Lien Hua agreed.

I'm kind of slow, I guess. We were halfway down the hall when it finally clicked.

"Hold on a minute!" I cried. "Now I just heard *you* say something, when *you* didn't say anything out loud."

Lien Hua shrugged. "Maybe you have déjà vu, too!" she suggested. "Wouldn't that be weird?"

"Déjà vu? But that doesn't let you read other people's thoughts!" I protested.

Lien Hua totally ignored me. "We could be psychic sisters," she said. "Cool, right?"

I didn't think so, and I wished she would stop smiling so much. I don't know which was creepier, her ESP, or her never-ending happy face! While I was thinking about that, she slipped away from me and disappeared down the hall, leaving me to go back to class alone.

I kind of dreaded walking into computer science by myself, twenty minutes late, and without a pass. I knew I was going to get in major trouble.

Suddenly, though, right outside the classroom door, Tina showed up and took me under her wing (so to speak).

"Hi," she said with a smile. "Lien Hua said you might have some trouble with Mr. Grady, so I thought I'd drop by and lend a hand."

I was a little surprised to see her there. "Don't you ever go to class?" I asked. Actually, she wouldn't be the first person. Have you ever noticed that in any school, there are always two or three people, usually eighth graders, who wander around the halls, and it seems like they never go to class at all? I always wondered how they got away with stuff like that. Tina, for example, seemed to be able to get away with doing whatever she wanted all the time.

She didn't answer me, by the way. She just threw back her head and laughed, as the light caught her gray eyes. "Oh, Jendra!" she said with a smile. Tossing her hair, she made a cute little fist and knocked on Mr. Grady's door.

When he opened it, Tina breezed in like a spring zephyr and dragged me through the door behind her. "Hey, Mr. Grady," she said, popping her gum. When I do that, it sounds really gross, but Tina did it with a kind of compelling charm. "Sorry we're late," she continued. "My dear friend Jendra and I were just bonding in the bathroom." She winked at him coyly. "You know—girl stuff? So is it okay if she just drops into your class now?"

Mr. Grady laughed, and let me assure you, that is extremely unusual. "Of course, of course," he said, smiling at me. I was getting so sick of seeing smiling faces. Fortunately, in that class I sit next to Leah, so I finally got a frown. A big frown.

"Why do you keep hanging out with Tina Sheperd?" she whined at me as soon as Tina slipped out of the classroom.

"She's my friend," I said. "I know you don't like her, Leah, but she's actually really cool once you get to know her."

"Chrystal got to know her," Leah said melodramatically, "and now she's dead."

I thought that was a little theatrical. "Chrystal's not dead," I said. "She moved to Australia."

Leah arched an eyebrow at me and asked, "Was that before or after she moved to Finland?"

I decided to change the subject. "Leah," I said, "do you believe in ESP?"

"You mean like mind reading?" she said. "Sure, I guess. Hey! Can you guess what color I'm thinking of? Or, no, wait! I'll guess you? Orange?"

"No," I said, "I—" She wouldn't let me finish, though.

"Pink?"

"No, but, Leah—"

"Green? Blue? Red?"

"Leah!" I exclaimed. "For Pete's sake, will you shut up about that! I'm not even thinking of a color. I just asked because I had the feeling earlier today that someone was reading my mind."

"Who?" she asked saucily. "Tina Sheperd?"

"No," I replied. "Just somebody else. Just somebody you don't know." I sighed. I was getting fed up with Leah, once again, so I decided to turn around and pay attention to our assignment—except I didn't know what our assignment was, and Leah was mad, so she wouldn't tell me.

I stuck my hand up in the air and waved it around for about half the period, until I finally gave up and just started surfing the Net instead. I'm not one to fret over missed classroom assignments. Besides, I was too busy fretting over my initiation at Jamey Fitzhughston's house that afternoon.

"Purple?"

That took me completely off guard. I pulled my head out of my locker and saw Leah standing next to me expectantly.

"That's it, isn't it?" she said triumphantly. "You were thinking of purple, weren't you?"

I was sick of her bugging me, so I just said, "Yeah, that's it. Purple. Wow." And then finally she went home for the afternoon and shut up about it.

Meanwhile, I wasn't sure what I was supposed to do. I figured just jumping on the bus wouldn't be a good idea since I was supposed to go to that initiation thing. And besides that, I don't ride the bus. But I've always wondered what would happen if I just did one day. I know they say that you can't ride unless you start at the beginning of the year, but if

59

he bus door screaming and crying
, would they really turn me away?

hinking about that when I happened to
ght into Jamey Fitzhughston, who was really
the person I wanted to see.

"Oh, Jendra, good," she said, sounding like she wanted to puke all over me.

"Hi," I said shakily. "Is it time for the initiation?" I was a little nervous about that. I could still remember my sixth-grade volleyball initiation, which involved stuffing lime Jell-O in my bra, and taping ostrich feathers to my face and Coke cans to my butt. And the people in charge of that little romp had actually liked me. I shuddered to think what someone who hated me as much as Jamey Fitzhughston did would make me do.

Actually, though, she didn't seem to want to make me do anything. In fact, she didn't want to have anything to do with me. In fact, even though she said my name, I'm not even sure she recognized me right away. As soon as she did, she got this disgusted look all over her face and left, so I was just standing there all by myself in the hall.

Until Tina showed up with a ready stick of gum. "Just ignore Jamey," she said, popping the gum into my mouth. It was spearmint this time.

"I think she hates me," I said.

"She does," Tina assured me.

"Well, that's comforting!" I exclaimed with a snort.

"Jendra," said Tina, rolling her eyes, "don't snort, for heaven's sake. It's so porcine."

"It's what?" I croaked.

She didn't answer me. "And don't worry about

Jamey, either. She may look fierce, but her powers are relatively weak."

"What?" I thought that was kind of an odd thing to say, but Tina stopped talking then and led me off down the hall.

"Where are we going?" I asked her after a few minutes of walking.

"Back to the bike rack," she said with a smile. "But first we'll stop by the vending machines to pick up some diet sodas."

"And some chocolate from the snack machines?" I hoped.

"Jendra," she said, rolling her eyes. "Fattening?"

"Okay," I said glumly.

Before long we were at the bike rack in back of the school. I felt a little bit out of place because everybody had a bike but me. Since we lived so close, I usually walked to school. Or sometimes Leah's mom gave me a ride, when it rained and stuff.

"You can ride with me," Lien Hua volunteered. "Unless you'd rather run along beside us."

Call me crazy, but that suggestion didn't sound too fun.

"My dog likes to do it," Lien Hua reasoned as she continued to smile. "But it's probably better if you get on the bike. You can sit on my handlebars."

"Are you sure?" I squeaked. That didn't seem like such a great idea to me. I mean, Lien Hua is pretty short, and my butt is pretty big, and frankly, I thought that if I sat on her handlebars, she wouldn't be able to see anything at all. But we didn't exactly have time to think of a better plan because the next time I looked up, I saw that the other girls were all pedaling away.

"Come on," Lien Hua urged with that smile of hers. "Hop on."

I hopped on, and the bike fell over.

"Okay," said Lien Hua with a giggle, "we can try again."

By the time we actually got to the wall around Jamey Fitzhughston's house, we'd been on Lien Hua's bike for about an hour, and we'd fallen over twice and run over a discarded pizza box, after narrowly missing a low-flying pigeon.

"Well, here you two finally are," said Tina, sounding exasperated. "Hurry up, Lien Hua. Everybody else is already inside." She rolled her eyes at me. "Jendra," she said. "We are going to have to get you a bike."

"Yeah," I said, trying to walk straight. My butt was really sore from the handlebars. "That sounds like a good idea to me. So, when does my initiation start?"

"As soon as we get inside," she said. I expected her to stroll up the front walk, but instead, she jumped over the wall. I suddenly glanced up at the house and noticed that something about it was strange. It didn't look lived in. The grass in the front yard was really overgrown, and vines covered the house and the wall.

"I thought you said this was Jamey Fitzhughston's house," I said, scrambling over the wall after Tina. I'm not much of a scrambler, and by the time I got to the other side, I felt a lot like scrambled eggs. Between riding the bike and scaling the wall, I was feeling pretty worn out. But, unfortunately, I still had a full afternoon ahead of me.

"Technically, it's an abandoned house," Tina explained. "But Jamey's the one who found it, so we say it's hers. We use it as our official off-campus headquarters. Once we get enough money, we're going to buy the place."

"Where are you going to get enough money to buy a house?" I asked.

Tina shrugged. "Why do you think we do all of those bake sales?" she asked.

That shut me up for a while. Tina led me around to the back of the house, to an old wooden door painted black. She stuck a diet soda tab in the lock and fiddled around with it until the door opened.

Inside, I expected to find an abandoned, messy old dump, but to my surprise the place was completely furnished—and furnished really well, I might add. Beautiful, intricately woven oriental carpets covered the polished hardwood floors, and the walls were painted metallic gold. From the shine you would have thought it was real gold. There were crystal chandeliers and a bunch of busts and statues and sculptures all over the place.

"Wow!" I said. "This is really beautiful. Where did you get all the money to decorate this? More bake sales?"

Tina only laughed. "Follow me," she said. "Oh, and, by the way, Jendra, take off your shoes."

I slipped off my black sneakers and stepped lightly across the elaborate rugs, following Tina into the kitchen. She suddenly stopped at the oven.

"Well?" I prompted. "Where to now?"

To my surprise, Tina opened the oven door and ordered, "Get in!"

"What!" I shrieked, jumping back a few feet. I mean, literally, a few feet. I sort of crashed into the sink, which hurt my butt even more, I might add. What was this? The old Hansel and Gretel treatment? "Okay," I said, "I've heard of weird initiation rites before, but do you really—"

"Jendra," Tina said shortly. "It's not what you think. Just get in."

I still felt shaky about the whole thing, but Tina slid in first, so I sort of had to follow her. To my surprise, the oven didn't have a back. Instead, it had a huge opening, that led to a spiral staircase.

"Whoa!" I said, carefully following her down the stairs. "This is really weird."

"Just wait," Tina said with a grin. "You're not going to believe your eyes once we get to the bottom."

11
Beyond the Secret Door

When the staircase finally stopped, I found myself standing in a tiny little room, barely big enough to turn around in. The air was sort of heavy like in a dungeon or a swamp. And it was very, very dark inside.

"So what now?" I asked, feeling really overwhelmed. "Where to?"

"The canal," Tina said, and I suddenly realized that the black, ripply place in front of us was running water, not a wall.

"Oh, my gosh!" I exclaimed. I jumped as a raft floated by. There wasn't much room for jumping around in that space, so, leave it to me, I jumped all over Tina.

"Watch it, Jendra," she said. "We'll work on your cheerleading moves later. Just get on the raft."

We both climbed aboard, and Tina picked up a long, wooden pole and started to push us forward.

"This is really weird," I said. "It's like something you would see in a creepy old horror movie."

Suddenly Tina stopped poling and knelt down at the side of the raft. She dipped her hand into the water, and then stood up and sprinkled a few drops of it on my head. "Do you swear silence and secrecy?"

"To what?" I squeaked, ruining her solemn ceremony. My voice was sounding ultra high for some reason. Maybe because I was nervous.

Tina sounded exasperated with me again. "Just say yes, Jendra!" she exclaimed with a sigh. "It isn't that hard!"

"Okay," I said, feeling dumb. "Yes."

"If you betray our secret, Death will seize your soul!" she finished spookily.

"Hey!" I yelped. "That's severe. You didn't tell me a threat like that was coming, or I might not have said yes."

"Just shut up and everything will be fine," Tina assured me shortly.

We ran out of water just about then, so Tina pulled our raft over to the bank, and we got out on a tiny piece of ground. There wasn't much room to stand again, and it was still really dark. In fact, all I could see was a big green door, at least three times as tall as I was, with big brass bolts all over it. I didn't know what was beyond the door, but something must have been pretty hot in there because steam was spraying out all along the sides.

I cocked an eyebrow suspiciously. "What is this?" I demanded. "The door to Hell or something?"

"Close," said Tina, which wasn't very reassuring.

"What' s making all that steam?" I asked.

"You'll see," Tina told me. With much less effort than I would have expected, she tapped on the door three times in the middle and it opened up.

Suddenly I was met with the shock of my life.

All the cheerleaders were in there, sitting on the ground in a circle, eating Pop Rox. That was a big enough shock by itself because I hadn't seen anybody eating Pop Rox in at least five years, and I was just pretty darn sure that they didn't even make them anymore. But that was nothing compared to the real surprise.

In the middle of the room, there was this huge— and I mean *huge*—glass case. It was at least nine feet tall, maybe taller, and it was extremely shiny. In the center, on a golden shelf, sat a single green and black pompon.

"Uh, not to be rude," I blurted out uncomfortably, staring at the pompon. "But what's that?"

Tina's gray eyes flashed brightly. With a slow smile that gradually got bigger and bigger, she announced theatrically, "The sacred pompon!"

"The sacred pompon?" I squeaked.

Lien Hua stood up and came over to me. "You know, the sacred pompon! We worship it!"

"Wicked, huh?" said Jamey Fitzhughston, who seemed glad that I appeared to be so horrified.

"Actually, I was thinking more of evil," I said uncomfortably.

Tina burst out laughing. "Evil?" she said with a giggle. "Oh, Jendra, don't be silly. The pompon is a thing of goodness. It protects us from the evils that attack."

"Evils?" I repeated suspiciously. "What kind of evils?"

"Jendra," said Tina. "Please, please don't be so naive. You may not believe this, but there are dozens of groups at school that are hostile to cheer-leaders. Their most intense desire is to destroy us. But thanks to the pompons, they can't do that. And that is why we've built the pompons a sacred shrine."

They all smiled, and I wanted to run away. My parents are pretty conservative, okay? They're so strict they wouldn't let me pierce my ears until I turned twelve, so I only shudder to think how they would react to sacred pompons. I knew I definitely had to get out of there and fast. I tried to think up some excuse.

"Uh, excuse me," I blurted out instantly. "But I think I have appendicitis!"

Tina grabbed me by the arm. "Nice try, Jendra," she said. "But don't be scared. There's no reason for you to run away. The ceremony hasn't even started yet."

"Ceremony?" I repeated flatly.

"Your initiation," Jamey Fitzhughston reminded me, and I felt my stomach sink.

"Oh, yeah," I said faintly. "That. Great." I walked around nervously for a minute before somebody finally pulled me down so I could sit with the rest of them.

"It's kind of hot in here," I said. "Is anybody else hot?"

"The pompon generates heat when we gather for a ceremony," Tina told me solemnly.

That explained the steam around the door, but I

still had a lot of unanswered questions. I just kept staring up at the pompon in the glass case. It was really pretty in a way.

"Gorgeous isn't it?" said Tina. "You know, it has given us great wisdom. The pompon can give you wisdom, too, Jendra, if you'll only join us."

That sounded kind of ominous to me. I tried to remember the techniques for resisting peer pressure they had taught us in our D.A.R.E. program, but I was drawing a complete blank. After all, there's a big difference between a police officer pretending to try to sell you drugs and a cheerleader really trying to get you to worship a pompon. Although, come to think of it, I guess both scenarios are pretty strange. But the point is, I had no clue how to escape.

"You worship this pompon?" I asked in disbelief. My mouth had fallen open so wide it must have looked like I had some kind of freaky degenerative disorder. "So," I said slowly, "this is like—a cult?"

"No," Tina assured me smoothly with a big grin. She must have noticed how freaked out I looked. I couldn't hide it. "No, Jendra, think of it more like a club."

"Like the baby-sitters' club," added Lien Hua helpfully.

"Exactly," said Tina, "like the baby-sitters' club—but . . . not." She smiled brightly. "Understand?"

"Not really," I said. "It still seems an awful lot like a cult to me. So, what do you guys do here?"

"Pray to the pompon and ask for her wisdom," Tina replied.

Oh, no! This wasn't a cult! Where could I have gotten such a silly idea?

"*Her* wisdom?" I repeated, arching an eyebrow. "Are you trying to tell me that this is a *female* pompon?"

"Of course," Tina told me. "Why do you think pompons always travel in pairs? They definitely have genders. This pompon is named Athena, to honor the Greek goddess Athena, patroness of wisdom, the olive, defensive warfare, and cheerleaders."

"Cheerleaders?" I repeated suspiciously. "I don't remember that last one from our ancient mythology unit."

Tina waved that aside. "Well, Jendra, you're only in seventh grade," she said with a shrug of her shoulders and a roll of her eyes. "Nothing you've learned up to this point is really true."

"Okay," barked Jamey Fitzhughston, holding up a brown paper bag, "we've wasted enough time. Let's get started. Today we're going to pray for poor old Chrystal, while we perform a ceremony to send her uniform into another dimension." She pulled the hideous coyote suit out of the bag, unlocked the glass case, and set the suit on the shelf next to the pompon.

"You don't mind about the uniform, do you, Jendra?" asked Tina innocently. "We'll have to get you another one or something. But the secret rites must be heeded."

"Yeah, whatever," I agreed even though I had no clue where she was coming from with that. I'm not real big on secret rites, you know? "Listen, can I leave?" I knew they wouldn't like that, but I didn't want to stick around and play the virgin sacrifice.

"Not yet," Tina said. "If you're really scared of Athena, you can wait on the raft while we finish the ceremony."

"Okay," I said. I don't know if she expected me to

do that or not, but that's what I did. It only took them a few minutes to finish, and when they did, Tina rejoined me on the boat.

"You can come back inside now," she said, tugging on my sleeve. "It's time for your initiation."

"Oh, great," I groaned. I sort of had to follow her. I really didn't have much choice.

"So what do you want me to do?" I asked, standing expectantly in front of "Athena." The mascot uniform, I noticed, had disappeared.

"Take off all your clothes," Lien Hua told me immediately. "And then hop around in a circle three times, while you sing the Barney song!"

What? I exclaimed. That didn't sound like much of a secret ceremony to me.

"Lien Hua!" Jamey whined, slapping her. Lien Hua was lying on the floor giggling wildly, so I kind of figured she hadn't been serious.

"Just ignore her, Jendra," Tina assured me. "Really, it's much, much simpler than that. All you have to do is cut off a lock of your hair and place it next to the pompon."

What? I exclaimed again. But nobody slapped Tina, and she didn't start giggling or anything, so I figured she had been serious.

"But why do I have to do that?" I demanded.

"Because," Tina said, making it sound as simple as slice and bake, "you're the new mascot. You and Chrystal both wore the coyote costume, and now you must bond in spirit by merging cells in another realm."

"What?" I shrieked. I didn't particularly want to bond with anybody in spirit. Especially not with somebody who had just been spirited away to Australia.

"Jendra, just put your hair on the shelf!" Tina snapped with a heavy sigh, like I really tried her patience a lot or something. As if all that was just business as usual to me.

"I don't have anything to cut it with," I said.

"That's okay," said Tina. "Here." And at that instant both Jamey and Lien Hua whipped out a pair of scissors and started hacking away at my hair.

"Aaah!" I screeched.

"Oh, sorry," said Lien Hua. "I guess I cut a little too much."

"Me, too," admitted Jamey. I wondered if she'd done it on purpose.

In horror I felt my head. Not only was my hair completely uneven now, I also had a huge bald spot right in the center of my scalp.

"Sorry," said Lien Hua.

"You moron," Tina scolded. "Now we're going to have to fix her hair."

"I hope so," I said.

Tina was watching me expectantly, so I took a handful of hair over and set it inside the case. I wondered if something phenomenal was going to happen next, but nothing did.

"Jamey and the others can finish up here," Tina said, grabbing my hand. "I'll take you back up the stairs now for punch and cookies."

"Punch and cookies?" I repeated slowly. I had seen a lot of freaky, freaky stuff that day, and as much as I liked Chips Ahoy, I really didn't think they would be much of a cure-all. And I didn't want any punch, either.

Basically, I just wanted to go home.

12
The Cheerleaders' Conclave

When we got upstairs, Tina tried to fix my hair, but it didn't do a lot of good. I still ended up looking like a French poodle gone mad, especially after she stuck a stupid little bow in my hair to cover up the bald spot.

Tina wouldn't let me leave until I had at least tried the punch and cookies. "Sit down, Jendra," said Tina, "and breathe, for heaven's sake."

They did have a very nice dining area, I'll give them that. We all sat around a polished mahogany table, and Lien Hua went into the kitchen and brought back a plate of homemade chocolate-chip cookies. I wondered how they baked them without an oven. It also surprised me that since Tina hardly ate any food at lunch, she did eat chocolate-chip cookies and drink peach-flavored Crystal Lite, which was what we were drinking. In honor of Chrystal, I guess.

"So, was that all there was to my initiation?" I asked hopefully.

"Pretty much," Tina said and handed me a napkin. "You've got chocolate on your nose," she said.

"Yeah, well, I've also got a dog bow in my hair," I reminded her.

"Now that the ceremony is completed, Jendra," said Jamey Fitzhughston, "you're officially one of us."

"One of whom?" I asked.

Tina tipped her glass and told me, "You're officially a member of the cheerleaders' conclave."

"The what?"

"You know, our conclave," Lien Hua explained, "like a secret council or something. Kind of like student council, but . . . not. Get it?"

"Sure," I said, taking a sip of my drink and feeling uneasy. "So, besides worshipping some pompon named Athena, what do we do at the cheerleaders' conclave?"

"Whatever we want," Tina told me, demurely munching a cookie. "Mainly, we decide what we'll allow to go on at school and what we'll forbid."

"You have that kind of power?" I asked in surprise.

"Of course," Tina said.

"Tina has a lot of influence over Mr. Talbert," Jamey Fitzhughston informed me, "so he has to do whatever she tells him . . . or else."

That sounded ominous. "So, you probably told him not to say anything about Chrystal's disappearance, huh?" I guessed. I had been wondering why an announcement hadn't been made to the student body.

"Exactly," Tina said. "We don't want word to get out too quickly. The basketball boys have got to be behind the whole thing. I'm sure Lien Hua told you how they were harassing Chrystal. One of them must have found out about our secret ceremonies to Athena and Ares. Religious prejudice is an ugly thing, Jendra. It turns ordinary people into monsters."

"Ares?" I repeated in confusion. Then I said, "Wait a minute. Let me guess. That's the name of the other pompon."

Tina nodded, and Jamey Fitzhughston added, "Named for the Greek god of war."

"So where is this Ares?" I wondered. "Does he have his own pompon case, or what?"

A hush fell over the room, and I got the feeling that I'd said the wrong thing.

Finally Tina pulled out a tiny piece of pompon and informed me gravely, "This is all that's left of him."

"Wait a minute!" I cried in recognition. "That's the piece of pompon I found stuck to the bottom of Mr. Talbert's shoe. Isn't it?"

"Yes," Jamey Fitzhughston cut in sharply. Sounding very menacing, she concluded, "Somehow the basketball boys must have stolen the pompon and then destroyed it because it's completely gone. It's nowhere. You can't trust them. You can't trust any of them. They're out to get us, and now that you're one of us, they're out to get you, too."

"Me?" I squeaked in terror.

"You will help us, won't you, Jendra?" Tina said.

She sounded a little unsure of herself, but even I had sense enough to know that it was probably a big act. "Without you we'll be doomed."

"Doomed?" That sounded eerie. "Why?"

"Because if our squad doesn't have a mascot," Lien Hua chirped, "we won't be able to participate in the Pompon Follies."

Somehow, that was anticlimactic.

"What's the Pompon Follies?" I wondered.

"Only the biggest cheerleading competition in the entire universe," Jamey Fitzhughston said. She added darkly, "And this year we're going to win."

"Athena will give us the power," noted Vanessa, one of the girls who hardly ever talked. As I stared into her gray eyes, she added, "You want to be part of our victory, don't you?"

Just then Tina's gray eyes flashed in the lamplight, and I suddenly became aware of something. "Hey! All of you guys have gray eyes!"

"You finally noticed," said Tina. "They're contacts. Our sacred eye gear. I'll pick you up a pair before school tomorrow. You can hardly even feel them."

"But I don't need contacts," I protested.

"Of course you do," said Lien Hua. "Your eyes are blue, which is close, but no cigar."

"So," I said. "Now that I'm a member of your conclave and everything, what happens? I mean, do I get some kind of mystical power or something?"

"Yes," Tina told me. "As a matter of fact, you do. We all have a special gift, thanks to the goddess gray-eyed."

Mine is telepathy! thought Lien Hua. *And Jamey Fitzhughston can breach the interdimensional gap!*

"Will you cut that out!" I complained.

"Is she communicating telepathically again?" Tina asked with a sigh. "Lien Hua can be so annoying when she does that. And I get sick of seeing her smiling all the time, too. That charges her powers, you know. The movement of her facial muscles releases a special chemical into her brain. If I felt like it, I could use telepathy, too. But I can't stand smiling so much."

"What about everybody else?" I asked.

"Deidre has the gift of prophecy," said Tina. "Vanessa can hypnotize people, especially teachers. Amber can talk to birds, and LaKaisha can make herself invisible. Both Jennifers can fly but only during daylight. Kyla and Erica can see into the sixth dimension but only after dark. Mitzi can zap stuff with her eyes, and Leigh can do those really high kind of kicks where you do the Chinese splits at the end."

"Hey, yeah," I said, "I was wondering how you did those."

"It's nothing," said Leigh modestly. "Do you want another cookie? Mitzi can always zap some more dough with her eyes."

"No, thanks," I said, "but what about Tina? What's her special gift?"

"Tina has all gifts," said Jamey Fitzhughston mysteriously.

She can do whatever she wants, added Lien Hua. Then she realized she was doing it again, so she wrinkled her nose and went, "Oh, sorry!"

"So what's my gift?"

The cheerleaders all stared at me for a minute. Then they stood up and got in a big huddle and whispered, so I couldn't hear them.

Finally Tina pulled back and informed me with a smile. "Jendra, we have decided to give you the gift of dance."

"Dance?" I repeated.

"Right," she said. "Didn't you tell me you couldn't dance? Well"—she fixed her gray eyes on mine and finished—"now you can."

13
More Bad News

"**W**hat's with your hair, Jendra? You look like a poodle." That was the first thing Leah said to me Friday morning in algebra.

I just shrugged. "I got a haircut," I said. "Kind of unexpectedly. I wanted to look like Jennifer Aniston. This is the way she's wearing her hair now."

Leah rolled her eyes and batted her eyelashes a few times for good measure. "Sure," she said. "Right."

"It's true," I lied. "I read it in *Seventeen*." But, fortunately, Leah wasn't interested in my hair anymore.

"Jendra, I'm worried about Mrs. O'Donnahee," she said. "She hasn't been to school for two days now, and it's not like her to be absent."

"Maybe she's sick," I said.

"Jen, she *never* gets sick."

I shrugged. I wished Leah would shut up. I had a lot on my mind. "Well," I said, "maybe one of her kids is sick."

"Jendra, she doesn't have any kids."

I tried again. I like to keep Leah happy, and she doesn't make it very easy. "Okay. Then maybe her dog is sick."

"Her dog? Jen, she doesn't have a dog."

"Well, fine," I snapped. "Maybe she bought a dog and then it got sick, okay? Gosh, Leah, how in the heck am I supposed to know? I'm just guessing here."

Just then an office aide slipped into the room. When I looked up, I noticed that it was Lien Hua.

Hi, Jendra, she said as she continued to smile. *Can you come here a minute?*

"Stop doing that!" I snapped.

"Stop doing what?" Leah whined. "Jendra, you are acting really weird today."

I looked to see what Leah was doing. "Stop writing your name on your paper," I said, trying to sound irritated. "I hate it when you do that."

"What?"

"Excuse me," I told her, heading for the door in a hurry. As soon as I got there, Lien Hua grabbed me by the arm and pulled me out into the hall.

"Bad news," she said aloud. "Mr. Talbert is dead."

14
Gray Eyes

I followed Lien Hua to the principal's office. "So what are we doing now?" I asked. "Calling the police?"

"Nah," Lien Hua said, sticking out her tongue for some reason. "Tina doesn't like the police to get involved. We'll probably handle it ourselves."

"Ourselves?" I squeaked. "What do you mean—handle it? Handle what? Did he just die? Did he die here at school?"

"I think so," Lien Hua said coolly, like it was no big deal at all. "We can handle it, though. We always have before."

"*Before?*" I was sort of shocked.

"Yeah," she said, continuing to smile. "Remember when the band director ran off to Wyoming last year?"

"Yeah," I said. "So?"

Lien Hua shook her head. "Uh-uh," she said with a knowing wink. "Wyoming? I don't think so. Maybe the cemetery in Wyoming," she said, yanking me into the rest room.

"What are we doing in here?" I asked as she practically threw me against the sink.

Lien Hua continued to smile. She seemed really happy for some reason, despite the fact that Mr. Talbert was mysteriously dead. "Here," she said. "We got you a present." She reached into her chain-mail purse and pulled out a tiny little box. I knew right away it had to be my gray contacts.

"Put them on," Lien Hua urged. "They'll look great on you."

I wasn't so sure about that, but I humored her anyway. I thought that was best. Actually, since my eyes are already blue, the gray contacts didn't make a real huge difference. I just looked sort of washed out, that's all, like in a bad picture.

"Oh, you look great!" Lien Hua chirped in delight, clapping her hands and jumping up and down. "Okay. Now we have to get to the office. Tina's waiting for us."

15
Emery Board of Doom

As a matter of fact, Tina was waiting for us. And under the circumstances she seemed relatively calm.

"I suppose Lien Hua told you about Mr. Talbert," she said, running an emery board across a perfectly manicured nail. "By the way, those gray contacts look great on you."

"How did Mr. Talbert die?" I asked, feeling nervous.

"The light above his desk fell on his head," Tina told me.

I winced in horror. "What?" I wailed. "Oh, no! That's terrible. How on earth did something like that happen?"

Tina shrugged. "Beats me," she said with a laugh. "You know the architecture in these new buildings.

83

It's so shoddy!" Like she was trying to prove it, she leaned against Mr. Talbert's office door, and it fell over with a huge bang. I looked at the hinges and saw that they had snapped in half.

"It was probably built in the sixties," Lien Hua said with a casual smile. "All the doors at my house do the same thing."

"They do?" I said flatly. That sounded weird to me.

"Yeah," she said. "I think it's because they're made of aluminum instead of steel. Right, Tina?"

"Most likely," she agreed.

Suddenly Mrs. Ellis, one of the secretaries in the office, yelled, "Is everything okay back there, sir?"

"Of course," Tina called sweetly in a deep masculine voice, that didn't sound like it could possibly have come out of her body. In fact, she sounded exactly like Mr. Talbert. I was stunned.

"How did you do that?" I squeaked.

"Tina has all gifts," Lien Hua reminded me.

"It's great fun," Tina said with a laugh. "I used to make tons of money at summer camp doing impressions of the counselors."

Suddenly, though, things weren't so funny. I turned and saw that Mrs. Ellis had gotten up from her desk and was now making her way toward Mr. Talbert's door.

"Oh, no!" I shrieked, pointing at her. "Look!"

"Oh, her?" said Tina, not batting an eyelash. I watched in amazement as she stuck out her emery board and pointed it at Mrs. Ellis. A green and black zigzag, like skinny lightning, shot out of the end of the emery board and zapped poor old Mrs. Ellis right between the eyes. She fell down and started twitching, as if she had been struck by lightning or eaten the cafeteria meat loaf or something.

"Mrs. Ellis!" I cried in horror, dropping to my knees. "Tina, what did you do to her?"

"Nothing really," Tina told me, tossing her hair. "She's just stunned. She'll snap out of it—eventually. Really now, Jendra, I can't have her parading into Mr. Talbert's office—she'd find his body for sure."

"Do you mean you haven't told her he's dead?"

"Of course not," said Tina. "I haven't told anybody. Except Lien Hua and Stephen, of course, because he's filling in."

"Stephen?"

"You know," she said. "Dr. Murphy. The science teacher."

Lien Hua informed me, "He is a fellow follower of the goddess gray-eyed. He's almost as Athena-crazy as we are. It's really cool."

"So, is he in the office right now?" I wondered.

"No, not quite yet," said Tina. "He's got to wait until he finishes his Chem. II class at the high school. Besides, the office is still all messy with guts and stuff everywhere."

"Guts?" I said. "I thought he was hit on the head." I peeked around the doorway. The office looked pretty clean to me, and I didn't see any sign of a body. Maybe Tina was blinding me with her psychic powers or something.

Before I could get a really good look, though, Tina grabbed me by the shirt and yanked me back through the door. "We have to clean up," she said.

I was afraid that was going to be my job since I was low man on the totem pole, but, fortunately,

Tina didn't mention anything about that. She just handed me a small metal lunch box. It must have been really old because it was decorated with the original cast of *Star Trek*.

"What, exactly, is this?" I asked, raising an eyebrow at Mr. Spock, who returned the gesture.

"Sacred stuff," Tina told me. "For the ceremony tonight. Guard it with your life."

I was afraid to ask what ceremony that would be, but I did start to lift the lid to see what was inside. Tina practically screamed at me, *"Don't open it!!!"*

"Okay," I said, slowly backing up. "Okay. Sorrrry."

"Oh, and Jendra," said Tina as I started backing out of the office. "One more thing. Try to stay off your feet as much as possible. You'll be dancing at the ceremony tonight."

"Dancing?" I chirped.

"Yeah, you got the gift, remember?" Tina reminded me. "You haven't used it yet, but don't worry, it's there. You won't need to practice. It will be entirely out of your control."

Lien Hua leaned over and informed me, without opening her mouth once, *You'll start dancing automatically whenever anybody says the word* hungry.

"Hungry?" I said out loud, wrinkling my nose.

"Hungry," Tina repeated. Then, all of a sudden, I started dancing. At first, it really scared me. I mean, I had absolutely no control over my feet. They just started flipping around, and I had no choice but to follow them.

"What am I doing?" I wailed in terror as I danced like a maniac.

"I'm not real sure," said Lien Hua, biting her lips.

"It looks like the Charleston. But, anyway, you'll stop whenever anyone says the word *turkey*."

Immediately my happy feet took a rest. "Turkey?" I repeated, staring at her. "Are you insane? You mean I start dancing whenever anyone happens to say *hungry,* but I can't stop until somebody says the word *turkey?* That's not fair."

"Relax," Tina said. "You'll hardly even notice the difference. Besides, you won't be doing any more dancing until the ceremony tonight." She smiled playfully, "Unless I say . . . *hungry!*"

Right away I went into a strange version of the funky chicken. "Turkey!" I yelled helplessly at the top of my lungs. "Turkey! Turkey! Turkey!" But for some reason I kept on dancing. "Hey!" I hollered. "What?"

"It doesn't work if *you* say it," Lien Hua told me with a laugh. Then she added, as a pun, "You turkey."

I stopped dancing and took a deep breath.

"Don't worry, Jendra," said Tina. "You'll probably make it through the rest of the day with no problem."

But I wasn't so sure about that. I was positive that a lot of people were going to be hungry at lunch.

16
Hungry Turkey

I already know what you're thinking. You probably figure that I went to lunch, and right away, somebody complained about being hungry, and I started busting a move all over the place. Well, sorry, but *wrong*.

Actually, I made it through lunch rather incident free, because I spent most of it eating pretzels with the cheerleaders. I did stop by Matt and Leah's table for a minute, though, which turned out to be sort of a mistake.

Instead of saying "hi," Matt greeted me with, "I wish I had some lunch money. Man, I'm hun—"

At that point I knew I had no choice. I had to cut him off. Clapping a hand over his mouth, I said in my gushiest voice, "I love you, too, honey." Then I ran across the cafeteria as fast as possible. After

88

that, all these rumors started circulating through the school that Matt and I were going out. Wonder why.

Anyway, the rest of lunch was a breeze because Tina and the cheerleaders sure didn't want to blow my cover.

Unfortunately, Texas history was next, and I've never yet spent a period in that class that didn't end up being unfortunate in some way.

At least Matt and I didn't have any problems getting back into class. Tina had definitely worked her magic. Ms. Long acted like she didn't even remember what had happened the day before. It was like she had never kicked us out of class.

Still, I was really worried that something would go wrong.

Sure enough, just as Ms. Long had dimmed the lights to show us her award-winning slides of the Alamo, some idiot blurted out, "Lunch was over too soon, man. I am so hungry!"

"Nooooooooooooooooo!" I wailed in agony, but it was too late. A split second later I was up on top of my desk, strutting my stuff. Disco this time.

"Jendra?" Matt croaked in alarm. "What the heck are you doing?"

I tried to be cool. I thought maybe if I played it just right, I could turn my mad dancing fetish into a trend, so I threw my hands up in the air and started clapping and yelling, "YMCA. Yeah. Yeah. Yeah. Yeah. YMCA!" Okay, so I don't exactly know the words, or the tune, and my voice is not exactly the greatest, so, come to think of it, this really wasn't one of my better plans. Plus, right away some smart-alecky guys in the back of the room started to sing their own off-color version of the lyrics.

"Boys!" Ms. Long interrupted in horror. She immediately ran to the other side of the room and flipped on the light.

"Jendra MacKenzie!" my teacher raged at me. "Get down from there this instant! What are you thinking of!"

"I know this looks bad!" I exclaimed, doing some moves from that old seventies movie *Saturday Night Fever.* "But I can't help it!"

"Go to the office at once!" she screamed.

"The office?" said Matt. "Are you sure you shouldn't send her to a disco?"

"Perhaps you don't like my slide shows," Ms. Long said to me crisply.

I had to think about that one, "Well, yes," I said, kicking up my legs can-can style as I jumped from desk to desk, "that's true. But that's not why I'm dancing. I promise, I can't help it! I'd stop if some-body would say *turkey.*"

"Turkey?" Ms. Long repeated suspiciously. Instantly I stopped dancing and fell off the desk. The *Star Trek* lunch box, which I'd been holding in my hand, landed on the floor beside me with a clatter. I started to kneel to pick it up, but before I could, Ms. Long swept down from on high and seized it in her talons. Then she soared back up to her nest and started puking up earthworms to feed to her young. (Sorry, I was just trying to use an extended metaphor. I won't do it again.)

"Ms. Long!" I said, grabbing for the lunch box. "I really need to hold on to that. Can I have it back, please?"

"No!" she yelled. "Are you insane? Go to the office!"

"But I need—" I started to protest.

Ms. Long interrupted me. "You need to learn some manners," she said, ruffling her feathers and flapping around the room. Okay, sorry. I did say I'd drop the bird metaphor.

"Can I at least pick it up after school?" I begged.

"No," she snapped instantly. "I'll be holding on to it for the rest of the year."

"For the rest of the year?" Oh, no! The cheerleaders were going to kill me!

"Please, Ms. Long," I whined. *"Please."*

"I'll think about it," she said coldly, fingering the latch.

"No!" I screamed, charging forward so that I crashed into her and we both fell backward against the window. Good thing it wasn't open, or we would have been lawn decorations. I jumped back to my feet and said, "Ms. Long! Whatever you do! Please! You can't open that lunch box."

"Why?" she demanded. "What's in it?" She narrowed her eyes suspiciously and guessed, "Drugs?"

"Drugs?" I exclaimed. "Do I seem like the kind of person who would have drugs?"

The whole class burst out laughing.

"Well, frankly," Ms. Long replied, "yes."

"You can't open that lunch box," I insisted. I tried to think of some reasonable excuse. "The hospital scheduled me to be an organ donor, and one of my kidneys is in there. Honest. Some guy needs it for an operation this afternoon."

"Miss MacKenzie," Ms. Long began cynically, but **just at that** moment thick coats of green slime started dripping down the seams on the sides of the lunch box. It landed in clots on the floor.

"Gross!" yelled Matt. "Jendra, what's in there?"

"I don't know," I told him. Actually, I was beginning to feel a bit concerned. I decided to go get Tina. "Excuse me, I've got to go to the office now," I said. Without waiting for a reply, I dashed out the door and took off down the hall.

17
Disaster!

What was happening to my life? It was like I had somehow entered *The Twilight Zone*. And what had been in that lunch box anyway? Was it really somebody's kidney? I shuddered at the thought and hurried to the office, hoping to find Tina.

She was there, all right. So was Dr. Murphy.

The first thing she said when she saw me was "Hungry." While I was dancing up a storm, the next thing she said was, "What happened to that lunch box?"

"What lunch box?" I asked pathetically.

"You know what lunch box," she replied suspiciously. "Where is it, Jendra?"

"What was in it?" I asked, tangoing around the office. That, at least, made it hard to look her in the eye.

93

"You'll find out at the ceremony tonight," she said. "Now where did it go?"

I groaned as I started break dancing on the floor. "My teacher took it away," I admitted.

Tina seemed mildly horrified. "Stephen," she said to Dr. Murphy, who was now sitting behind the principal's desk. "What are we going to do? Oh, for heaven's sake, Jendra, will you stop dancing? You're driving me nuts."

"Well, it's not my fault," I told her, jumping on top of the late Mr. Talbert's desk to do a cute little tap-dancing routine. "I feel like I'm stuck in some stupid Shirley Temple movie. I warn you, I might start singing 'On the Good Ship Lollipop' any time now."

"I always liked that one," said Dr. Murphy, humming a few bars.

"Turkey!" Tina shouted. "Turkey! Turkey! All right?" Usually Tina was so calm and cool. She was definitely much more upset than I had ever seen her before. "Stephen, what should I do?" she wailed.

"You'll have to go and get it," he told her.

"Yes," said Tina, half closing her eyes. "The pompon will help me." Suddenly she dropped to her knees and lifted her face to the ceiling. "Athena!" she called loudly. "Hear my cry and answer my call of distress." Then she rolled her eyes back in her head for a few minutes. She looked weird.

"Listen," I said. "I've got to be getting back to class now." I started to move toward the door, but just then Tina jumped up, all energized, and blocked my path.

"No!" she said. "Not alone! The pompon has given me wisdom. I will accompany you."

I had kind of dragged my feet on the way to the

office, so by the time we got back to the classroom, Texas history was over. I knocked timidly on the door before Tina boldly led me inside. Ms. Long was sitting behind her desk, grading papers. I didn't want to talk to her, but I sort of felt like I had to say something.

I hoped she'd look up, so I just stood there quietly. Finally I worked up the nerve to clear my throat softly, only it ended up being much louder than I'd intended, and for some reason I sneezed at the same time.

Ms. Long looked up and saw me there. "God bless you," she said. It must have been Tina's influence.

"Thanks," I told her. "Hey, listen, Ms. Long, I know I shouldn't have behaved so badly in your class. But . . ." I looked down. Then I blurted out, "Could I please have my lunch box back?"

Ms. Long seemed surprised. "Your lunch box," she said slowly. "Didn't I already give it to you?"

I exchanged a worried glance with Tina. "Noo," I said. "I'm pretty sure I would remember."

"Oh, that's right," said Ms. Long, remembering. "I gave it to Leah."

I felt my heart stop beating. "To Leah?" I repeated flatly. That was bad news.

"Yes," said Ms. Long. "She stopped by my desk after class and said she wouldn't mind picking it up for you. That was awfully nice of her. Of course," she said reflectively, "maybe she was just hungry."

She shouldn't have said that.

"We have to go," Tina said as I danced out the door. "Thank you for your time."

Out in the hall Tina immediately whispered, "Turkey!" and then said to me, "Jendra, this is terrible.

How could you let your stupid little friend get her hands on that lunch box? Didn't you know how important that was?"

"There's no need to panic," I said. "Leah just picked up the lunch box to give it to me. And we have computer science together next period. You know, Mr. Grady's class. I can just go and get it from her now. It's no big deal."

Tina sighed heavily. "Let's just hope she didn't open it," she said darkly.

"Why?" I wondered again. I was really dying to know. "Tina," I said, "what's in it?"

Tina looked worried. "Mr. Talbert's toupee," she said.

"His toupee!" I exclaimed in horror. I almost fainted right there in the hall.

"And his false teeth, and some green slime," she finished, adding, "it's not as bad as it sounds, Jendra. We need them for the memorial ceremony tonight. Mr. Talbert's ghost might jinx the Pompon Follies for us if we don't have a decent memorial ceremony for him."

"We're going to have to have a memorial ceremony for Leah if she opens that lunch box!" I exclaimed. "She'll completely freak out! I mean, this is Leah, the girl who totally lost it when she found a cigarette in her brother Brian's saxophone case. A bunch of slimy dentures will definitely send her over the top."

"Well, hurry up, then," Tina urged me. "Go to your stupid class and get the lunch box back before she can open it."

That's just what I did. Well . . . at least it's what I tried to do. But when I got to Mr. Grady's class, I made the shocking discovery that Leah wasn't there.

"She had a dentist's appointment," Mr. Grady informed me. "Her mother picked her up a few minutes ago. Is there something wrong, Jendra? Jendra?"

I didn't have time to stay and chat. I tore out of the building as fast as I could, with Tina right behind me.

18
Dive-bombing Downward

*T*ina and I stopped for breath at the foot of the flagpole at the front of the school. Once we got there, we bumped into Lien Hua, the Jennifers, Amber, and someone else I couldn't see.

"Hey, ow!" that someone said.

"Sorry," I said, looking around in concern. "Who did I step on?"

"Oh, that's just LaKaisha," Lien Hua told me with a smile. "She made herself invisible again. She's always doing that."

"Lien Hua, wipe that stupid smile off your face," said Tina. "This is serious. Our brilliant young mascot here just lost Mr. Talbert's toupee."

Lien Hua gasped. "And his dentures?" she asked in concern and held her breath.

"Gone," Tina assured her. "Just like the green slime. This is a total disaster."

"But who would steal dentures?" asked LaKaisha. It was weird to hear her voice without seeing her face. It was kind of like watching a dubbed Japanese movie. Well, actually, it wasn't really like that at all, but I was just stalling because I don't like this next part of the story, so I'm trying to take my time getting to it.

"Mr. Talbert's toupee and dentures," Tina told them, "which, incidentally, we need for tonight, are in that *Star Trek* lunch box. I gave it to Jendra for safekeeping. But somehow she lost it. And now her whiny little friend Leah has it, and she's in a dentist's office somewhere. Jendra, do you know what dentist she goes to?"

"No," I said blankly.

Tina threw a fit. "What?" she shrieked. "Do you mean to tell me that she's your best friend, and you don't even know a thing like that?"

"Well, jeez, I'm sorry, okay?" I said. "I also don't know the name of her vet, or which brand of toothpaste she prefers. There are some things that just never come up in conversation."

"She should use Colgate," said Lien Hua with a smile. "It has less sugar than the leading brand, and that means it's less fattening."

"Oh, who cares about that," snapped Tina. "We've got to get those fake body parts back!"

"Ow!"

"Oh, sorry, LaKaisha."

Suddenly Amber decided to say something, which was a big deal, since I had never heard her speak before. "That bird knows where she went," she declared, pointing to a cardinal, sitting on top of the flagpole. "He saw her leave just a few minutes ago, didn't you, Red?"

"Oh, that's right," I remembered, "Amber can talk to birds."

"Well," said Tina. "Where did they go?"

"To Newman Dental," Amber replied, after listening to the bird chip for a few seconds. She was an amazing interpreter. I don't speak bird, of course, but it takes me at least two hours to translate a sentence out of Spanish, so I was impressed.

"Which way?" Tina asked.

"The bird doesn't know street names," Amber replied, "but he can take us there."

"Oh, yeah," I quipped. "That would be real convenient—if we could fly." Then I suddenly remembered that the Jennifers could fly. Cozying up to Athena did have its perks, I guess.

"Just hold on to my neck," Jennifer Martinez said to me. Tina, of course, could fly by herself. I mean, she could do everything, after all. Just as Jennifer and I were taking off, Lien Hua jumped on Jennifer Rosmand's back. The Jennifers and Tina flew with almost no effort, and they didn't seem to have any trouble following the cardinal.

"I can't believe I'm doing this," I said. "This has got to be, by far, the strangest thing I've ever done."

"Just wait till tonight," said Tina. Then she started screaming. "There it is! There it is! Down there! See? Newman Dental!"

We went dive-bombing downward, awing the onlookers in the parking lot. Jennifer Martinez landed on the roof, which was a bit inconvenient, but at least she got us there in one piece.

Unsteadily, I scrambled down a fire escape on the side of the building to join Tina, Lien Hua, and the other Jennifer on the sidewalk.

"Okay," said Tina. "Now, this doesn't have to be difficult. All we really need to do is waltz in there, find Leah, and nicely ask her for the lunch box. I only pray that she hasn't lifted the lid yet."

I was praying for that, too, because I got the feeling that if Leah had seen something she shouldn't have, Tina would do anything necessary to shut her up.

We probably looked a little strange, parading into the office single file especially if anyone had followed us in from the outside. Probably not many of Dr. Newman's patients fly in.

While the Jennifers distracted the receptionist, Lien Hua, Tina, and I split up and started searching for Leah. After accidentally stumbling into the men's room, I finally found her in the third room on the left.

I decided to talk to her alone, so she wouldn't get suspicious. I'll admit, I was pretty nervous when I shoved open the door. Fortunately, though, Leah was lying there, with a laughing gas mask covering her mouth and most of her nose. When I went in, she sat up, took off the mask, and said, "Jendra!" She was probably pretty surprised to see me there, in the middle of school and everything.

"Hi, Leah," I said, smiling weakly. "Any cavities?"

"Uhm, excuse me," said Dr. Newman, sounding annoyed. "Do you have an appointment?"

Just guessing here, but I think what he meant by that was, *Who are you, and why don't you leave my office before I call a security guard?*

"I'm Leah's stepmom," I said. I tried to look indignant, so he would believe me. But I wasted my effort there. Boy, was that guy ever a cynic!

"Perhaps you should talk to your friend at a more appropriate time," he suggested.

"Just take the lunch box, Jendra," Leah said with a sigh. "That's what you came for, right?"

"Right," I replied slowly, glancing around the room. "Thanks."

"No problem," Leah said. "But about that lunch box . . ."

I caught her eye, and for a minute I was afraid she was on to us. But then she just smiled and said, "It's over in the corner, under my coat." I let out a sigh of relief, grabbed the lunch box, and headed for the door.

Dr. Newman was obviously glad to see me go.

19
After Dark

"Everything is okay," I said out loud, trying to convince myself. "Leah didn't look inside the lunch box, so when I give it back to Tina, everything will be fine."

But everything didn't feel fine. I had a very hard time walking calmly out to the reception area when I knew what was inside that lunch box. For one thing, even though Leah hadn't said anything, I wasn't convinced that she hadn't peeked inside the lunch box. I mean, what would she have said after finding Mr. Talbert's toupee and dentures packed in green slime? I can't think of an appropriate remark, can you?

Anyway, despite my general feeling of creepiness, I handed the lunch box back to Tina, and we went outside. We all flew back to school, just in time for the last five minutes of computer science. It's a good thing I wasn't in there for very long, because I really couldn't concentrate.

I passed Matt on the way to my locker after school. He gave me kind of a funny look.

"Jendra," he said. "I'm kind of worried about you."

"Worried about me?" I squeaked with a nervous laugh. "Why?"

"Well, for starters there's your hair," he said. "No offense, Jen, but I think that poodle cut looks really weird on you. And then there was that little dance performance you gave in Ms. Long's class, not to mention the fact that your eyes have suddenly turned gray."

"Oh, is that all?" I said, forcing a laugh. "Well, don't worry about me, Matt. I'm a cheerleader now, right? And basically, all that stuff just sort of goes with the territory."

Matt looked skeptical. "Well, whatever," he said. "But, Jendra, I should warn you, Tina can be really rotten sometimes. I just hope you never catch a glimpse of her dark side."

I hoped so, too.

"I'll be fine," I assured him, not feeling fine at all.

Then, to my horror, he suddenly said, "Listen, Jen, do you want to come with me to the principal's office? I need to ask Mr. Talbert some stuff about the science fair."

"Uh . . . I think the science fair's canceled," I blurted out nervously, running off down the hall. I ended up running right into Tina.

"Jendra," she said, gray eyes wide. "Calm down. Why are you so worked up?"

"Why am I so worked up?" I repeated incredulously. I sighed. "Tina! Do you know Matt wants to go and talk to Mr. Talbert? And I'm sure he's not the only one. What is going to happen when everybody finds out that he's dead?"

"Don't worry," Tina assured me. "We've already taken care of that. Nobody will ever know. We thought up the perfect cover story, okay? We're telling everybody that Mr. Talbert moved to New Guinea to be a missionary and that Dr. Murphy will be taking over until he gets back."

"But," I protested, "don't you think that people are going to get the tiniest bit suspicious if he never comes back?"

"Well, that's not our problem," Tina said with a sigh. "I'll be in ninth grade next year. Now go home and get some sleep, Jendra. You need to be rested for the ceremony tonight."

"Why do we have to have the ceremony at night?" I wondered. "I mean, I think that shrine to Athena is creepy enough in the daylight. After dark it must be terrifying."

"It's awe-inspiring," Tina said with a smile. "You'll love it."

"I doubt it."

She slipped me a stick of gum and said, "No, Jendra, really you will. Now go home and get to bed. And don't worry. When it's time for the ceremony, we'll contact you."

"That's what I'm afraid of," I mumbled, slowly chewing my gum.

20
Disturbing Dreams

As far as I know, nobody ever said that eating chicken-fried steak gives you weird, disturbing dreams all night, so my mom's cooking can't be to blame for all the strangeness that started the second my eyes slid shut.

But all I know is, no sooner had my head hit the pillow than I heard a tiny little voice in the back of my brain whisper, *Jendra. Jendra. Don't go to the ceremony tonight.*

"Where *should* I go?" I mumbled, squeezing the sides of my comforter.

Confidentially, I was hoping for France, which has been my dream ever since I read about Joan of Arc last year in exploratory French. Kind of goes along with that whole sidewalk café thing I mentioned earlier.

The voice had other ideas, though. *Don't go to the ceremony,* it said a second time. *If you dance there tonight, you'll never dance again.*

"Good," I grumbled with a snore. "I hate dancing, anyway."

Sounding exasperated, the voice snapped, *I don't think you get it, Jendra. You're in a lot of trouble.*

Suddenly another voice practically screamed, "Save me! Help me! Get me out of here!"

In an instant an entire scene flashed before my eyes. I don't quite know how to describe it, but there was this beach, and it was covered with tents, and bodies, and soldiers with swords, and then off in the distance there was this big, walled city.

A second later the image flickered out and a girl's face abruptly appeared. She was really young, not much older than me, and she looked totally hysterical—the way Leah looks when you make her use butter instead of low-fat yogurt spread.

"Help!" the girl sobbed. "Please help me! Get me out of here! I didn't do anything! I'm innocent!"

Her voice was so shrill that with a sharp gasp, I sat up sweating in my bed, suddenly wide awake. Then I looked at my clock.

"I've only been asleep for five minutes?" I groaned. "No way! When are those stupid cheerleaders going to summon me?" I eyed the window suspiciously and wondered if they'd come in that way. After all, it wasn't like them to use the door.

Nobody was there, though, so feeling annoyed, I fell asleep again.

Before long, I felt this floating feeling, like I was flying. And I saw myself hovering over the physical science room, where I took a seat in the back row. I turned to the girl sitting next to me. She was blond and tiny and dressed in prep clothes.

(Oh, and by the way, I was dressed up like Peter Pan with webbed feet—but somehow I really don't think that's important to the dream.)

"What are you doing here?" I asked her, suddenly recognizing her. She was the same girl who'd been screaming her head off in my other dream.

"I'm failing physical science," she explained with a shrug. "But Dr. Murphy said that if I redid our last lab, he'd let me slide by with a seventy. So I came in for tutorials. Tina helps me a lot."

She nodded toward the front of the room, where I saw Tina in her cheerleading outfit peering over a petri dish. She was holding a pompon in each hand.

Meanwhile, in the other corner of the room, Dr. Murphy was busy playing mad scientist. This was a little game where the scientist uses spaghetti tongs to dip prisms into a bubbling vat of chemical soup. From the stench, I was guessing the soupy glop was Dr. Murphy's own secret recipe.

"He's so weird," my new friend whispered as she nudged me.

"No kidding," I replied in an Italian accent as I realized I'd forgotten my locker combination. (Again, probably unimportant details.)

Just then, though, something *really* bizarre happened. Dr. Murphy lifted a soup-soaked prism from his stew pot just as an exceptionally bright sunbeam shone in through the window.

As the light passed through the prism, we were dazzled by a blinding white flash—like white pepper thrown in the eyes.

Speaking of eyes, I rubbed mine for a full sixty

seconds. Then, as soon as I could focus again, I saw a pair of twelve-foot-tall translucent beings standing by the soup pot in full armor.

Everyone in the room was shocked into silence.

After a few seconds Dr. Murphy sort of squeaked out, "Are you here to make up a lab?"

"Silence, mortal!" boomed one of the visitors. She moved menacingly closer to Dr. Murphy and bellowed, "Who dares summon the spirits of Athena and Ares?"

"We were in the middle of battle," the other being snarled. He didn't look much like the nice, friendly type to me. For starters, he was holding a bloody spear, which was kind of a turnoff. His eyes burning, he finished savagely, "And I would have won."

The female being burst out laughing.

"I would have!" her companion insisted indignantly.

The goddess laughed again. Even harder this time. And then she noticed Tina.

"Girl," she began, sounding interested, "you look athletic. Which god do you serve?"

Tina looked blank. Finally, sounding flustered, she managed to say, "Well, my mom was raised Methodist, but my father is Catholic, so I guess I serve—"

In confusion the goddess interrupted, eyes narrowing into two slits, "Not Aphrodite?" As she asked the question, the room shook like thunder, and I could tell that everybody pretty much had their fingers crossed that Tina wasn't a big Aphrodite fan.

Fortunately, she said, "No, I've never even heard of Aphrodite."

She's such a good liar, I thought. I mean, come on, even *I* have heard of Aphrodite.

The goddess smiled. "How nice," she said and then asked, "Is there a temple of Athena nearby, by chance?"

Knowing Tina, she was probably planning to lie again and say yes, but dumb ol' Dr. Murphy just had to butt in. "The ancient Greek gods aren't worshipped here in twenty-first-century America," he said.

There aren't really words to describe the goddess's reaction, so I'll just put it this way. Athena did not take that well.

Ares, meanwhile, started storming around the room, smashing stuff—beakers, Erlenmeyer flasks, test tubes. Glass was flying everywhere. I winced and wondered if Dr. Murphy would note that on his inventory sheet and make him pay a fine at the end of the year.

Just as Ares was about to move on to breaking *animate* objects, Tina suggested desperately, "Of course, we could always start a temple."

Again, Athena smiled. (Ares didn't, though. He just kept right on breaking stuff, but since Athena was talking, we all just kind of ignored him.)

"Worshipping me will have its rewards, girl," Athena announced. "I will make you my priestess, the head of a sacred cult. And I can offer you powers, special powers, powers that will enable you to accomplish whatever you desire. . . ."

Suddenly the scene changed, and I was back at the cheerleaders' shrine, eating cookies and drinking Crystal Lite.

I heard myself asking, "What's the Pompon Follies?"

"Only the biggest cheerleading competition in the

entire universe," came the sinister reply. "And this year we're going to win."

"Athena will give us the power."

Immediately back in the science room, I saw Athena levitate Tina's pompons into the air. She and Ares then each extended a single finger and sent forth two surges of power—I could see them—like bolts of lightning. The pompons took on a life of their own then and began to glow.

Then the gods were gone, and Tina was standing beside me, talking to the other girl in the back of the room. She obviously couldn't see me.

"You saw them, too," Tina said. "And we can't pretend you didn't. But don't worry. We'll make room for you on the squad. You can be our mascot. Okay, Chrystal?"

The scene changed again.

I still saw Chrystal, but now she was in the shrine, backing away from the rest of the cheerleaders in terror.

"I didn't do it!" she shrieked, sounding desperate. Her eyes were wide, and one of them was bright blue. Somehow she'd lost a contact.

"Liar!" Jamey Fitzhughston snarled. "I saw you! You betrayed us!"

"No!" she shrieked, even more desperately than before. "It wasn't me! It wasn't—I swear! I don't know what on earth happened to it, but, honestly, I didn't take it!"

"She's lying," I heard Jamey say as the scene changed again. "How can you possibly believe her? Ares disappears and some seventh-grade nobody just happens to find a piece of him stuck to Mr. Talbert's shoe? She's lying, Tina."

Pacing the floor nervously, Tina demanded, "LaKaisha, are you sure nobody saw you with the mascot suit on?"

"I made myself invisible before I put it on," she insisted.

Sinisterly, Jamey said, "That didn't stop Mr. Talbert from figuring out it was you who stole his pants and loafers. He knew those basketball players weren't serious about wanting his pants and shoes. And he figured out that we were responsible for what happened to Chrystal, too."

"We shouldn't have tried to frame the basketball boys for Chrystal's disappearance," Tina decided. "Pinning that malicious note to the mascot didn't make the basketball team look guilty like we planned. It just made us look suspicious. And that stupid wad of phony death threats you showed to Jendra, Lien Hua, I'm sure she saw right through those. She must know we got rid of Chrystal."

"We'll have to do more than scare her now," Jamey Fitzhughston said darkly. "You're right, Tina, she knows. And we've got to do something to keep her from talking."

You see? pleaded the voice that had called my name before. *Now do you get it? Don't come to the ceremony, Jendra. Your life may depend on it! Stay asleep!*

So, naturally, just then I woke up.

21
Dancing in the Darkness

I'll admit, that kind of took the edge off my night's sleep.

After that, I did have one brief dream about getting trapped inside a gigantic banana split. I only mention it because I think it might be symbolic somehow. Like maybe the ice cream represents fear of the chill darkness, and the nuts and bananas stand for my state of mind at the time. Or maybe I was just having a sugar craving. Who knows? When I woke up, I was chewing on my pillow.

That wasn't all I was doing. Almost as soon as my eyes slid open, I jumped to my feet and started bouncing up and down on my bed, doing the Texas two-step.

"So that's how they're planning to summon me," I said to myself, dancing over to my bedroom door.

It's times like this when I'm glad I have my own room. Fortunately, my evil twin brothers, Mason and Cooper, who share a room down the hall, sleep like rocks. I had begun to boogie-woogie down the hallway toward the stairs, and was making plenty of noise, too, but neither of them even opened an eye.

Noisily I hoofed it down the stairs and then slid out the front door and toddled off down the street toward Jamey Fitzhughston's house and the shrine to the pompon Athena.

Should I be honest? I didn't want to go. I had this funny feeling in the pit of my stomach. Well, not a funny feeling so much as an ache. And not in my stomach so much as in my feet, because even with my gift, I still wasn't the most graceful dancer, and I kept stepping all over myself. But what I'm trying to get at here is that I was scared. And even though I kept telling myself, "That was only a dream," I couldn't shake my sense of dread—no matter how many times I shook my bootie.

I'm sure I must have looked like a total lunatic, or at least, a Britney Spears wanna-be, shuffling down the street like that in the lamplight. Fortunately for my reputation, it was about two o'clock in the morning and none of the neighbors were up. For some reason, though, I had the eeriest feeling that somebody was following me. I didn't know why, exactly, but every time I turned around, I expected somebody to be standing there. Don't ask me who. But that feeling just wouldn't go away.

By the time I got to the sanctuary, I was doing that bizarre little dance from *Pulp Fiction*. You know the one I mean, right? Maybe you haven't seen *Pulp Fiction*, but don't worry, I haven't, either. I know the dance, though, because my cousin Amy saw the movie, and then she acted it out for me, scene by scene. Amy's kind of weird. I'm not, of course. I mean, I was just dancing down the street in the middle of the night. Nothing abnormal there!

Tina was waiting for me on the other side of the wall. "You know the way inside," she whispered.

"Sure," I said, following her through the scary black back door.

"Oh, by the way," Tina said and added "turkey." Finally I stopped dancing.

I thought I locked the back door behind me. At least, I was pretty sure I did . . . kind of . . . I mean . . .

Oh, well.

Tina had already disappeared by the time I got into the kitchen. Even though I had done it before, I was still totally nervous about climbing through the oven. But I didn't have much choice. If I didn't show up at the ceremony, the other cheerleaders would come and get me. I knew that for a fact. It didn't matter how bad I wanted out. They needed a mascot—so they needed *me*.

The oven seemed a lot darker than I remembered, and so did the staircase. And as if that wasn't spooky enough, I also thought I could hear somebody behind me, breathing ever so quietly. But then, whenever I turned around, the noise just stopped. So I figured it must be my imagination.

I had to cross the canal myself, which, I must say, I didn't enjoy. I felt kind of like Charon, the skeleton guy who rows across the River Styx. Of course, I didn't know what Charon looked like, so I formed a mental image of Karen, this annoying, whiny little girl I used to go to Brownies with back in second grade. Boy, Karen was a real brat. And it seemed like she always had a runny nose. And one time she slept over at my house, and when it was time for breakfast . . .

Just when I had gotten myself all worked up remembering that little girl Karen, I looked up and realized I was on the other side. Quickly I jumped off the raft and walked up to the steaming green door.

Nobody would dog-paddle across black, bubbling water, would he? I mean, that doesn't seem logical, right? So those swimming noises must have been my imagination, too. I sighed deeply and knocked on the door, three times in the middle, the way I had seen Tina do it.

After only a few seconds the door slowly creaked open, and I joined the rest of the cheerleaders inside. I thought I closed the door, but evidently I left it open a crack.

22
Confessions

"**H**ey, Jendra!" called Lien Hua with a smile. She was dancing around the room, shaking her butt. "Ready to do your ceremonial dance? Tina's got the toupee."

"And the dentures," said Jamey Fitzhughston darkly, pulling them out of the lunch box.

"Gross!" I exclaimed. "Put those away! They're disgusting."

"Jendra," said Tina in a reprimanding tone. "Are you trying to say our sacred ceremony is disgusting?"

"Well," I said slowly. "That wasn't what I was saying, but . . . yes."

Tina sighed and tossed her hair. "Well, we weren't asking for your opinion," she said shortly. "Now come over here so we can start the ceremony."

"I'd rather not," I told her.

"What?" Tina acted shocked that I would question something she said.

I tried to work up my courage. "I said I'd rather not," I repeated. "Tina, I don't know how to tell you this, but . . . uh . . . ." Finally I just spit it out, saying, "I don't want to be a part of the cheerleaders' conclave anymore."

"What?" Tina screeched. From its sacred place inside the glass case, the pompon seemed to stir. Then it started to glow with a strange green light. The room got even warmer than usual, and I began feeling really scared. The whole glowing thing made me remember that freaky dream—the dream about Athena and Ares in the science room, and I started getting kind of worried. I mean, what if it was true?

"Nothing," I said hastily. "Nothing."

Tina smiled slowly, and the pompon settled down. "Well, that's good," she said. "I wouldn't want you getting any crazy ideas. Jendra, that could be dangerous."

"Yeah," said Jamey Fitzhughston sinisterly. "We wouldn't want to have to do to you what we did to Chrystal."

"What you did to Chrystal?" I repeated, taking a step back.

"Jamey!" Tina exclaimed, glaring at her good and hard. "Stop. You're scaring her."

"Hold on a minute," I said. Now I was getting really worried. "I thought you said the guys on the basketball team were harassing Chrystal and made her leave." Just as I said that, I remembered that in my dream Tina had said, "We shouldn't have tried to frame the basketball boys."

"Tina," I began hesitantly, not quite sure how to

put it. "Were you completely honest with me about what happened to Chrystal?"

"Let's not talk about that right now," Tina said as she tossed Mr. Talbert's dentures back and forth between her hands.

"No, I think we *should* talk about it right now," I told her, feeling really suspicious. "If you guys did something sinister to Chrystal, I think I have a right to know. I mean, after all, I am her replacement."

"All right," said Jamey with an evil chuckle, "we did. There. Are you happy now?"

"No!" I exclaimed. I turned in the direction of the door, but Tina stopped me by grabbing my arm.

"Jendra," she said. "Don't get the wrong idea." Her voice sounded friendly, but her fingernails were sharp, and they were really digging into my skin.

"Ouch!" I yelped. "Tina, let go of me!"

"You can't leave yet!" Tina insisted. "Jendra, you don't understand. We had to get rid of Chrystal. She turned her back on the conclave. She was going to betray all of our secrets."

"What secrets?" I whined, trying to twist out of her grasp.

"Well, we wouldn't tell you now," said Jamey Fitzhughston, like I was totally retarded. "You just said that you wanted to leave. Besides, Chrystal did more than that. She also stole Ares. She stole him, and she threw him into the furnace. I saw her with my own eyes. She was a traitor."

"Yes," Tina agreed. "She was a traitor to the conclave, and that's why we banished her to another dimension."

"Another dimension!" I exclaimed in horror. "You

banished her to another dimension just because she stole some stupid pompon?" Just then I made a chilling realization. "Mr. Talbert was on to you, too, wasn't he? He figured out that you were the ones who stole his pants that day, and the ones who got rid of Chrystal. And so, you're the ones who—"

"Of course," said Jamey. "You didn't believe that old a-light-fixture-fell-on-his-head story, did you? That's the lamest excuse Tina's come up with in a long time."

"Tina!" I confronted her.

Tina sighed in exasperation. "Well, Jendra!" she justified. "We have to have a sacrifice! The pompon must be appeased!"

She turned to face the back wall, and I noticed for the first time that somebody was tied up in the corner. He wasn't wearing his toupee or his dentures, but still I was pretty sure it was Mr. Talbert.

"I don't believe this!" I yelled. "You weren't planning a memorial ceremony for Mr. Talbert at all. You had a much more sinister reason for needing his toupee and dentures. You were planning to banish him to another dimension."

"Sure," Jamey said. "Well, that or kill him. We were going to flip a coin."

Then suddenly I realized something else. The Twinkies. "You poisoned the whole basketball team with Twinkies, didn't you?" I said. "To make it look like they all took the day off so they couldn't be blamed for Chrystal's disappearance, which made them look doubly suspicious. And that means that I gave Mrs. O'Donnahee a poisoned Twinkie, too. It made her sick! And that's why you didn't want me to eat that Twinkie!"

"Well, that," said Tina, "and plus Twinkies are

really fattening. Did you know that Twinkies have a shelf life of twenty years? Now, honestly, Jendra, do you really want a big yellow hunk of saturated fat sailing through your veins? I saved your life!"

"Why, so you could sacrifice me?" I screamed theatrically.

"No," Tina said, trying to calm me down. "Why would we want to sacrifice you, Jendra? We only sacrifice traitors."

"And is Mr. Talbert a traitor?"

From the back corner Mr. Talbert was looking really worried.

"Mr. Talbert," said Jamey, "is a threat to our survival. We have to sacrifice him to appease the pompon. Don't you understand?"

"I understand you're all a bunch of psychos," I said, starting for the door again. I finally managed to twist away from Tina, but when I got to the door, I found that I was blocked by an invisible wall.

Running's no good, said the voice inside my head. *They'll only chase you. They might even push you into the canal. And then you could drown.*

"LaKaisha will never let you out," Jamey said ominously. She sounded really evil, and now I was starting to get scared.

"LaKaisha, let me go!" I screamed, banging into her temporarily transparent body with my fist. I'm telling you, LaKaisha must have been the girl of steel or something because she never budged an inch.

But then, when I looked past LaKaisha to the doorway, I saw a sight that horrified me, in every imaginable way.

"Leah!" I exclaimed, my eyes bugging out of my head.

Standing behind me, in the doorway, in her pajamas, wet from head to toe, was my best friend Leah Livingston, looking a little sleepy—and a lot scared!

23
Traitor!

"**L**eah!" I screamed. "Oh, my gosh! What are you doing here!"

"I followed you," she explained. "After I opened up your lunch box this afternoon and found those disgusting dentures and that slimy toupee, I figured that something was for sure wrong." She batted her eyelashes furiously. "Jendra, what's going on here?"

"Gee!" I said. "You sure picked a lousy time to show up!"

"Traitor!" Jamey yelled suddenly, charging forward. "You see, Tina?" she said. "I told you she was a traitor. Your little friend Jendra led a stranger to our sacred shrine."

"I didn't mean to," I argued. "She just followed me. I don't know how it happened."

"Well, it wasn't exactly hard," said Leah. "You were the only person out on the street, and you looked like one of the Rockettes. Just exactly why do you keep dancing like that, anyway?"

Glaring at me viciously, Tina declared, "Because she's so *hungry!*" Right away I started doing my own special version of the Mexican Hat Dance. I felt like an idiot, but I couldn't exactly do much about it. Meanwhile, Jamey Fitzhughston grabbed Leah and tied her up in the corner.

"Why are you doing this?" I wailed, stamping my foot rhythmically. "Leah and I didn't do anything to you!"

"You sent your friend to spy on our sacred ceremony," said Jamey Fitzhughston ruthlessly, "and the penalty for that is death."

"Death!" I squeaked, twirling around in a perfect pirouette. "That's a little harsh isn't it? Couldn't you just send us into another dimension like everybody else?"

For her part, Leah started whining and blinking her eyes so much I'm sure she couldn't see anything at all.

"Wait a minute!" I said in horror. "Death? Lien Hua, you said that the band director ran away to a cemetery in Wyoming last year." I turned on all of them savagely. "But you killed him, too. Didn't you?"

Tina looked confused.

"No," Lien Hua said with a laugh. "He really did move to Wyoming. I just made that up to be funny."

"Lien Hua!" I shrieked.

"Silence!" Tina commanded solemnly in a booming voice. She dropped to her knees and declared in an eerie voice, "We will ask Athena for her guidance."

"Athena?" Leah croaked.

"She means the pompon," I said, nodding toward the giant glass case. "Over there."

Leah's eyes just kept on widening until they were enormous. "Oh, my gosh!" she said. "Jendra, do your parents know about this?"

Meanwhile, Tina's head was tilted back, and for some reason, she was making these weird, other-worldly gurgling noises in the back of her throat. Abruptly she sat up and announced, "The pompon has spoken."

"Does she say to let us go?" I hoped as I bounced gracefully from one corner of the room to another.

"No!" Tina boomed. "She says that there must be a sacrifice."

Tina paced around me cagily. Suddenly she snapped her fingers and yelled, "Turkey!" As soon as I stopped dancing, Jamey hurried over and tied my hands behind me.

"How could you do this?" I wailed. "I thought you were my friend. Besides"—I suddenly remembered— "you can't kill me. You need a mascot for the Pompon Follies."

"We can always find another seventh grader just as gullible as you," Tina predicted ominously. "The Pompon Follies aren't until next week. Don't worry. Every girl at school is dying to be a cheerleader mascot." She cackled wickedly. "And there's just about to be an opening."

24
Judge and Jury

Just when I had all but given up hope, I heard that tiny voice in the back of my head assuring me, *Don't worry. I won't let Tina kill you. Just be patient. There's got to be some way you can escape!*

Lien Hua? I thought. Finally I recognized the voice, and for once I had brains enough not to yell, "Stop doing that!" It was Lien Hua all right. I saw her smiling at me from over in the corner.

But how can I get away? I thought back. *Tina's obviously going to kill me and Leah and Mr. Talbert tonight. How can I possibly stop her?*

There's always a way, thought Lien Hua. *Just leave it to me.*

Like I had a choice!

She smiled and then she said out loud, "Tina,

before the sacrifice, shouldn't we offer a ceremonial prayer to Athena?"

"A ceremonial prayer?" Tina repeated, interested.

"Yeah, you know," said Lien Hua. "We ought to pray that our sacrifice will be acceptable in her eyes."

"Sacrifice?" Leah whined in terror. "I don't want to be a sacrifice! I don't want to be anyone's sacrifice!" She batted her eyelashes like there was no tomorrow. "Get me out of here!"

"Shut up!" I told her. "Screaming's not going to do you any good."

So Leah tried whining. She seemed so pathetic, like a tiny puppy dog wearing too much mascara. I almost started crying myself, as a matter of fact.

"Jamey!" Tina commanded, sounding solemn. "Run to the utility closet and get me the ceremonial knives."

"You'll never get away with this!" I told her. I didn't know what to say, and that's what they always say in the movies. Then I thought of something else. "Why don't you go upstairs now, Tina, and leave the room for a few minutes?"

"Nice try, Jendra," Tina said tossing her hair, "but I've seen that movie."

"Really?" I squeaked. "What movie was that?"

"Shut up!" snapped Jamey Fitzhughston, giving me the evil eye.

I closed my mouth fast, but I was getting pretty worried and sweating pretty hard. The pompon shelf was starting to glow again, and I didn't like that one bit—believe me.

"Athena has spoken her divine word," Tina announced, climbing to her feet. Jamey returned from the recesses of the room with silver-tipped knives, daggers, and swords. That did not look too encouraging. Predictably enough, there were thirteen of them.

"You see, Jendra," said Tina, grabbing a long silver sword, "I'm the judge, and the verdict is guilty. The sentence, of course, is death." She stepped closer and drew the sword, pointing it at my throat. "Jamey," she bellowed, "how do I make the ceremonial cuts?"

"I don't know," Jamey whined. "Just kill her. We'll worry about the ceremonial stuff later. As long as she's dead, she can't cause any trouble. Just hurry up, Tina."

I shut my eyes tight and started saying my prayers. At first I couldn't really think of any prayers to say. Then I meant to start reciting the Lord's Prayer, but I was so nervous, I accidentally started reciting the Pledge of Allegiance instead. I get all that memorization stuff mixed up.

"Jendra!" Leah whined, wrinkling her nose. "What the heck are you talking about!"

"Oh, well," I decided with a sigh, "at least I'll die a patriot!"

I shut my eyes tight again, sure I was really done for. But all at once, Lien Hua came to my rescue by saying the one word that could set me free.

25
The Hungry Turkey Strikes Again

"**H**ungry!" Lien Hua yelled. "Hungry! Hungry! Hungry!"

Suddenly I leaped up and started doing these really high theatrical kicks. Fortunately, I kicked Tina right in the face, and she fell backward and landed right on her butt. She dropped the sword and clasped her chin in pain.

"Turkey!" she yelled, rubbing her swollen jaw. "What in the world is wrong with you? How dare you hit me?"

"Well, sorry!" I told her. "But you're the one who's trying to kill me, remember?"

Tina picked up her sword and lunged at me again. "This time you won't get away so easily," she said sinisterly.

"Hungry!" Lien Hua yelled again, and I did another fantastic kick. Just like before, Tina went sprawling backward on her butt.

Struggling to her feet, Tina growled, "I am getting just a little bit sick of this."

She hadn't said *turkey* yet, so I was just jumping around like a maniac, dodging the sword she kept swinging at me, which was pretty tricky because my balance was off with my hands still tied behind me. Just then, I heard a shrill shriek behind me and turned to see that Mitzi and the Jennifers had hacked off almost all of Leah's hair.

"Help, Jendra!" Leah screamed. "Help meeeeeeeeeeeeeeeeeeeeee!"

I would have, but I couldn't stop dancing, and besides, Tina was gaining on me with that sword. I kept looking out for Lien Hua, expecting her to do something else to help us, but I couldn't see her anywhere in the room. It was like she had just suddenly disappeared.

About that time Tina thrust the sword forward and stabbed it through the toe of my shoe. Fortunately, my black sneakers are about a size and a half too big, so she didn't do any toe damage or anything. Actually, I just kept dancing, and the shoe flipped off the point of the blade and flew through the air. To my horror, it crashed into the pompon case, breaking the glass.

"Oh, my gosh!" I exclaimed. I was getting pretty tired of jumping around the room like a Riverdance reject, but unfortunately, Tina was still jabbing with that sword of hers. And, over on the other side of the room, poor Leah sounded like she was being tortured.

"Aaaaaaaaaaaaaaaaaaaaaaaaaaaah!" she wailed.

I whirled around to see what was wrong with her, and I noticed that the other cheerleaders had ripped off her Doc Martens and thrown them into the canal. That was a mistake. I mean, those shoes are sacred to Leah. They're her most cherished possession, like her children or something.

I was scared to think what they would chop up next, so I danced over to the other side of the room and started crashing into the bloodthirsty cheerleaders.

"Where on earth did Lien Hua go?" I wondered as I knocked cheerleaders over left and right.

Tina, of course, was pretty angry by this time. "Listen, Jendra," she snarled, "I'm getting sick of this. You had better hold still so I can kill you."

"Do you even know how retarded that sounds?" I said, rolling my eyes.

"Turkey!" Tina spat out spitefully, and I dropped to the ground next to Leah.

Tina was gaining on us and the rest of the cheerleaders had flocked around us, looking as deadly as the most venomous killers that travel in a pack—cigarettes.

"This is it, Jendra," Tina told me, closing in on us. "Say your prayers."

But just then, I noticed feathers floating around the room, and I looked up to see a barn owl flying above us.

Letting out a gasp, Tina and the others dropped to their knees. "It is the goddess gray-eyed," Tina said. "She has honored us with her material presence." She took a deep breath and proclaimed, "We must stop to worship her. It's the real Athena."

131

26
The Great Escape

"*The real* Athena?" Leah whined to me. "What does she mean, the *real* Athena? Somebody needs to tell her that Athena is a fictional character."

"Shut up!" I said in a harsh whisper. "Maybe they'll leave the room."

"Now do you believe me?" whined Leah, batting her eyelashes, about the only bits of hair she had left on her head. "I told you, Jendra, Tina Sheperd is a bad influence."

"Silence, mortal," Tina ordered in a deep, eerie voice. "Who dares speak in Athena's sacred presence? We must all fall silent and listen to her divine speech."

"Divine speech?" Leah squawked. "That's a barn owl."

"Shut up," I whispered again. "Tina's got a sword

132

and a band of psychopaths on her side. You don't want to get her mad."

Suddenly the barn owl started flapping around and squawking a lot.

"Athena?" Tina asked in awe. "What is it, O divine one?"

To my surprise, the owl swooped in through the hole my shoe had made in the case, snatched up "Athena" in its talons, flapped out of the shrine, and flew out the green door.

"The sacred migration!" Tina exclaimed in that same eerie voice. "We will follow wherever you lead, O goddess gray-eyed!" Instantly all the cheerleaders chased after the owl, locking the door behind them, so that Leah and I were shut inside the shrine.

"See?" Leah screeched at me. "I told you, didn't I? What did I tell you about Tina Sheperd?"

I know it wasn't exactly an appropriate moment, but suddenly I just burst out laughing.

Leah started batting her eyelashes at me. "What is wrong with you?" she whined.

"Sorry," I said with a giggle, "it's just that you look so strange without your hair."

"Jendra!" she whined shrilly. "That is *so* not funny."

"Sorry," I said again. "What do you want me to do?"

"Well, you could start figuring out how to untie us and how we can get away," she said. "That barn owl can't go far, you know, up and down the canal. And you can bet those cheerleader friends of yours will be back. Aaaaaaaaaaaaaaaaaaaaaaaah!" she suddenly screamed in terror. She pointed up at the ceiling and exclaimed in a panicky voice, "Here comes one of them right now! Look!"

I looked up and spotted Lien Hua, climbing down from the top of the glass case.

As she jumped to the ground, I exclaimed in relief, "Lien Hua! Where on earth have you been?"

"I went to the zoo," she said with her usual smile.

"You went to the zoo!" Leah exploded indignantly. She was totally hysterical, and I can't say that I blamed her much. "We're here, in this sacred temple place, getting beat up and stabbed at by psychotic cheerleaders, and you're going to the zoo?!"

"Well, I had to get the owl," Lien Hua explained.

"What?" I said.

"Yeah," said Lien Hua. "That materialization of Athena?" She grinned as usual. "No way! That's just some dumb barn owl I stole from the nocturnal exhibit. But it will keep them busy for a while. Tina's always waiting for a materialization of Athena. I knew my little trick would work. Come on," she said as she knelt and untied my hands. "We've got to get out of here right away. Before they get back."

"Why are you helping us?" I asked, standing up while Lien Hua untied Leah and then Mr. Talbert. He was too confused even to speak. (Well, either that or he was too embarrassed to talk without his dentures.)

"Because I like you," Lien Hua replied, "and because I am getting so sick of getting rid of people for the sake of the pompon. I mean, first Chrystal, then Mr. Talbert . . ." She shuddered. "I'd hate to see you go, too. Now come on, hurry." She held out a hand, and we followed her to the base of the glass case.

"Do we have to climb up there?" Leah whined, wrinkling her nose in distaste. "I mean, it's so . . . evil."

"It's just a pompon case," said Lien Hua, looking at her like she was nuts. "Besides, it's the only way out. If we try to go back by the canal, Tina and the rest of them will get you for sure. And then it's R.I.P. for you two. It's not so bad. All you've got to do is hold on and climb."

Uneasily, Leah, Mr. Talbert, and I followed Lien Hua as she scrambled up the side of the pompon case.

"You know," Leah said, "I don't like this at all."

"Really?" I said. "That's weird. I'm having a blast. In fact, I'm thinking of taking my next vacation here!"

"Oh, shut up!" she whined.

"You always were the sarcastic one, Miss Mac-Kenzie!" Mr. Talbert declared.

With a wrinkled nose, Lien Hua asked Mr. Talbert with a weak smile, "You're not going to give us detention when we get back to school, are you?"

"Oh, no," he assured her. "For what you have done, you'll get something much worse than detention."

"Even after I saved your life?" she asked with a wounded smile.

"Hey, are you the one who made me have that weird dream?" I asked Lien Hua. She nodded.

"I can't believe I trusted Tina!" I exclaimed. "Why does everyone follow her so blindly?"

To my surprise, Lien Hua replied, "Because she

laces that gum she gives out with a mind-controlling chemical. Really, it's true. She keeps it in a box in the science storage room. Luckily, it's hard to chew gum when you're smiling all the time. Aren't you glad you have me on your side?"

"Yeah," I said, "but what I still don't understand is—"

"*Jendra*," Leah grunted, "could you maybe ask questions later?" She was in a hurry to get to the top. Plus, every time I opened my mouth, I ended up slipping and accidentally kicking her in the head. Poor Leah was having a rough night!

Just as we reached the top of the pompon case, we got an extremely unpleasant surprise. Tina and the gang suddenly filed back into the room, and Tina picked up her sword again. When they noticed that we had nearly escaped, they all started freaking out in a major way.

"They're getting away!" Tina screamed in outrage, pointing a finger at the ceiling.

Lien Hua grabbed a bronze ring that opened the trapdoor in the ceiling. "You're too late, Tina," she said, pulling down the door to open it. "The terror stops here. I'm going to help Jendra and Leah and Mr. Talbert get away!"

"Never!" Tina bellowed, and she started climbing up the case after us. Tina, we soon saw, was a really good climber.

"Oh, great!" Leah wailed. "She's almost at the top."

Lien Hua had already boosted herself through the trapdoor, and I was halfway through, when a few other cheerleaders started climbing the case, too.

"Oh, no!" Leah wailed, shoving my butt through the hole. "Hurry up, Jendra! Quit blocking the exit! I'm not about to be the one who gets stuck down here."

"I'm going as fast as I can," I assured her. I've never been much of a climber. I was that kid in grade school PE who always fell off the knot—at the bottom of the rope.

Suddenly I became aware that the pompon case wasn't as secure as it had been a moment before. I guess all the weight was too much for it. It started to shake a little, and then it started to wobble big time.

"Quick! Jendra! Hurry!" Leah shrieked as the case started shaking underneath her. "Let's get out of here! We've got to get out of here—now!"

I yanked myself up and out the door finally, pulling Leah and Mr. Talbert after me. Almost as soon as we got out, the entire case toppled over, crushing Tina and the other cheerleaders.

27
Return to the Scene of the Crime

Disgustingly enough, by Monday everything in my life was pretty much totally back to normal—except for the fact that Leah and I looked like a pair of twin pet poodles. Actually, she looked much, much worse than I did. I just had a big, gaping bald spot. *All* of her hair was gone!

"No way," said this girl named Rebekah who sits next to me in algebra. "I do not believe you."

"It's true," I told her. "Check out the latest issue of *Seventeen* if you don't believe me."

"But Jennifer Aniston's hair always looks so cool," she protested. "I can't believe she would be sporting that awful bald cut."

"Thanks!" Leah whined.

"Oh, ignore her," I advised Leah. "She's just jealous."

"Whatever," said Rebekah, turning around.

"Girls!" reprimanded Mrs. O'Donnahee from the front of the classroom. Yes, our teacher was back and in fine form.

"I still don't understand what made me so sick," she said.

"It was probably those Twinkies someone left in your box," I told her. "I mean, do you know that Twinkies have a shelf life of twenty years? Those things are just little yellow balls of cream-filled saturated fat, waiting to attack your arteries." I confidently pulled out a pack of gum (my *own* gum) and offered her a piece. "Here," I said. "This is much better for you."

"Jendra," she said suspiciously, "is that gum in my classroom?"

Mrs. O'Donnahee was a nut about gum, too. Who knew?

So it was back to the office for me. Pretty much business as usual.

When I got there, though, I was in for the shock of my life. The whole place was cordoned off with yellow tape, and there were so many cops swarming around, it looked like a policemen's ball. Well, I mean, actually, I've never been to a policemen's ball myself. I always have wondered, though, do the officers go in uniform? I mean, they would all look the same, right? And then, what do they do? Just dance around together? They would look like total idiots! Actually, I think it would be really cool if all the police officers went to the ball in disguise, dressed as firefighters. Of course, they'd have to steal the uniforms from the fire station, and that would be kind of bad if there was a fire that night. Anyway, it's probably not a really big surprise that I've never gotten an invitation to a policemen's ball. . . . But I guess I've kind of gotten a lot off the subject, huh? I should get to the point.

Police officers were all flocked around the office door before I saw them leading Dr. Murphy away in handcuffs. Mr. Talbert was standing outside the door with a satisfied smile on his face.

"Hey!" I yelped loudly. "What's going on?"

One of the officers turned around and told me, "Young lady, this man committed a major crime. We have reason to believe that he kidnapped your principal and poisoned some members of the basketball team with chemicals from the school science lab."

"Yeah, well, you're probably right about that," I told him at the same time that another officer went, "Gary, don't tell her all that."

As I watched them lead Dr. Murphy away in handcuffs, I called after them, "Hey, by the way, do you all have dates for the policemen's ball?" None of them answered, so I figured they already had dates.

Since the office was all taped off and everything, I decided to go back to class. On the way there, I stopped in the second-story girls' bathroom. Not that I had to go to the bathroom or anything. But have you ever noticed how in movies and books, the characters always go back to the place where the story started? I figured just to keep the literary tradition alive and everything, I should probably retrace my steps and go back to the good old bathroom.

"Yep," I said to myself as I stared into the mirror. "This is where it all started." I took a deep breath.

Then I realized that had been a major mistake. After I got done gagging, I decided I'd better head back to the classroom before Mrs. O'Donnahee came looking for me.

Just before I turned to go out the door, though, somebody fell on my head.

In case you're wondering if you read that wrong, you probably didn't. I said somebody fell on my head. I'm only repeating myself because I have this feeling that I might have lost a couple of people. I mean, that probably sounded pretty weird. (It didn't feel so great, either.)

For a split second of heart-pounding terror, I found myself staring into the sweaty face of a ferocious-looking blond eighth grader. (No simple seventh grader could have looked so ferocious.) Our eyes met, and she focused on me intently. One of her eyes was blue and the other was gray, but they were both blazing with a crazed gleam. For a minute I thought I was in for it. But fortunately, she whirled around and ran out of the bathroom and off down the hall without saying a word.

At first I was in total shock. I didn't know what to do. I searched the ceiling for some explanation, but this time not a tile was out of place. It was like a stray airplane had crashed down from nowhere and used the part of my hair as a landing strip. Well, technically, it was more like some weird girl had fallen on my head in the bathroom—in fact, that's exactly how it was. But the airplane simile was kind of nice, don't you think? Actually, I stole that one from Leah. She used it in a paper once—only she wrote about an ocean liner, not an airplane— and, of course, she wasn't comparing it to getting hit on the head by a falling girl. At least I don't think she was. She wouldn't have gotten a very good grade in that case because our papers were supposed to be about Paul Revere.

"If only Paul Revere were here right now," I murmured. Not that I'm such a big Paul Revere fan, but think about it. As an excuse for missing class, "A girl fell on me in the girls' bathroom" just wouldn't get me far. But "*Paul Revere* fell on me in the girls' bathroom"? Now, *that* might turn some heads.

Paul Revere didn't show up, though, so I figured the British weren't coming, or George Washington, or anybody else unexpected like that. And since I didn't really want to risk another encounter with that ferocious eighth grader, I decided I had nowhere to go but back to algebra.

"Sorry, Mrs. O'Donnahee," I said, sliding through the classroom door. "I can't go to the office. It's become a crime scene. And the bathroom's off-limits, too. People keep falling from the ceiling."

That was sort of an exaggeration, but it did get her attention for a second.

"What?" she said, taken off guard. But before I could explain, she got distracted by a fascinating little thing called the quadratic formula. I'm not sure exactly what this celebrated quadratic formula did, but it sure did take up a lot of room on the board, and it looked highly suspicious to me.

While Mrs. O'Donnahee played her mysterious little quadratic formula game, I leaned back in my chair and started drawing a picture of Olympian gods. I figured I could take it as a present to Tina when I went to visit her in the hospital that afternoon. That's right, even though the cheerleaders had taken a nasty fall, they weren't dead. They were just really, really smushed, but their shrine was pretty much destroyed.

Now, I know most people probably wouldn't have kept on being friends with Tina, especially not after she pulled that deadly sword trick, but I hated to let her just languish alone in the hospital. I mean, sure, she may have been evil and all, and, yes, she had tried to murder me, but still she was Matt's cousin. So I had to respect her for that.

Besides, what could possibly happen to me in a hospital room?

(For the answer to that incredibly stupid question, see the next chapter.)

28
Eerie Silence

Poor Tina.

She looked really pathetic, lying back on her pillows, staring at the TV monitor, watching some stupid orange juice commercial.

"Don't take this the wrong way," I told her, handing her my drawing and a "Get Well Soon" balloon, "but I really don't want to be a part of the cheerleaders' conclave anymore."

"Yeah," she said, glancing down at the casts on her broken legs, "I think you kind of made your point."

"Jeez!" I said. She was pretty injured. "How did you guys get out of there, anyway?" I asked.

"Fortunately," Tina replied, "the cracked place in the case landed on me, so I got crushed the least. The other girls weren't so lucky," she said. "Most of them are pretty bruised and broken, but we're all still kicking—except Leigh, that is."

"Leigh?" I repeated. "Didn't she have the power to do those really high—"

"Not anymore," Tina cut me off. "When the case fell over last night, the sacred shelf cracked in the middle. It was completely destroyed, and the pompon was lost. I think that stupid barn owl dropped it into the canal. So we lost all our powers. Now we're just ordinary girls." She sounded depressed as she confided, "You know, Jendra, that's no fun."

"At least you're still head cheerleader," I reminded her. "And you didn't get in too much trouble. Dr. Murphy got arrested this morning at school."

"I thought so," she told me. "Stephen was so careless. But we're in plenty of trouble, too, Jendra, believe me. Mr. Talbert's holding such a grudge that he's decided to break up the squad. Not only are we disqualified from the Pompon Follies, but Jamey, both Jennifers, Vanessa, Mitzi, Erica, and LaKaisha all have to transfer to other schools. And I'm supposed to spend my Saturday mornings talking to the school counselor. Can you believe it? Why would Mr. Talbert think I'm emotionally disturbed?"

"Maybe because you kidnapped him and tried to banish him to another dimension?" I guessed. I may not always pay attention in class, but sometimes an answer is obvious even to me.

"Like being banished to another dimension is so terrible!" Tina pouted.

She picked the wrong time to say that.

At that exact instant the door flew open and in charged that same ferocious-looking eighth grader who had fallen on my head earlier. Only this time she didn't look quite so ferocious. That's because she was wearing Doc Martens and a little white sweater set and a plaid skirt. She was still mad, though. Really mad.

"Being banished into another dimension isn't so bad, huh?" she screeched so shrilly that for a minute, I thought the barn owl was back.

"Chrystal!" Tina exclaimed in horror. Looking kind of scared, she flattened herself against her pillows and asked, "What are you doing here?"

"In this room?" Chrystal demanded sarcastically. "Or in this dimension?" She had a delicate, girly little voice, but she still seemed incredibly hostile. I was glad she wasn't mad at me.

Until I found out she was mad at me.

"You're the girl they got to replace me, aren't you?" she said, noticing me just before I could slip out the door.

"Uh, yeah," I said shakily. "And you must be Chrystal. I think we met briefly in the bathroom this morning. You fell on my head?"

"And you convinced the rest of them to banish me to that horrible realm," she said darkly, forcing me right up against the bed.

"No," I replied nervously. "I think you're a little confused about that. I'm just the replacement, and believe me, I don't want to keep the job. I've been having kind of a bad week."

"Were you kidnapped by Myrmidons on the coasts of strong-walled Ilion?" Chrystal demanded cynically.

"Well, no," I had to admit.

"Then don't talk to me about having a bad week," she said, glaring at Tina.

"Don't glare at me," Tina told her. "I only did what I had to do. You're the one who turned your back on us."

"Yeah, well, you're the one who sent me into another dimension!" Chrystal yelled. "Did you expect me to be your best friend after that?"

"You're awfully good at shifting blame," Tina replied, "when you're the one who threw the pompon Ares into the furnace. Jamey saw you."

I expected her to get even more upset, and maybe say something bad about Jamey, or declare that she was perfectly justified in burning up that evil pompon. But to my surprise, Chrystal looked shocked.

"What?" she exclaimed. "I never did that."

"Then where is it?" Tina demanded.

"Where's what?" said Chrystal.

"The pompon Ares!" Tina told her passionately. "If it hasn't been destroyed , then it's still out there somewhere. And that is really a big deal because that pompon has incredible powers. If it ever fell into the wrong hands . . ." Tina bit her lip. Then she asked Chrystal, "What *did* you do with it?"

"Nothing," Chrystal insisted. "I never took it. I don't have it."

In alarm Tina demanded, "Then who does?"

Suddenly it came to me. "Tina," I said. "What made you think that Chrystal stole Ares?"

"Well, Jamey told me," she replied. "And I just took it for granted . . ." Suddenly she caught on and gasped.

"Jamey!" she whispered in horror.

"Jamey?" said Chrystal.

I thought Tina might fall out of her hospital bed. "She was always jealous of my power," she said.

"She wanted to be more than second in command."
She turned to Chrystal. "So she stole the pompon
and framed you."

"It's true," Chrystal agreed. "I did see Jamey take
Ares out of the case one time, and I never saw her
put him back."

Tina looked terrified. "Why didn't you mention
this before?" she gasped.

Giving her the world's dirtiest look, Chrystal
replied flatly, "You banished me to another dimension, remember?"

"But if Jamey's got the pompon Ares," Tina said,
"that means she still has her powers. She can contact the war god. She can banish people to other
dimensions, she . . ."

With a sly smile I suddenly remembered. "She
doesn't go to our school anymore."

Tina grinned. "That's right," she said brightly.
"She doesn't."

We all had a good laugh about that one, until
Chrystal suggested, "What if she comes back for
basketball games?"

That was an alarming thought, and I'll admit it, I
wanted some reassurance from someone.

We all pressed close together and listened atten-
tively.

But all we heard was eerie silence.

About the Author

Sarah J. Jett was born in Nebraska City, Nebraska, in 1979. She lived in five different states and attended thirteen different schools before her family settled in Austin, Texas. Currently a junior at the University of Dallas in Irving, Sarah is majoring in English. Her future aspirations include pursuing a career in teaching while continuing her writing.

Sarah has been writing since she could pick up a pen, and before that she dictated stories into a tape recorder. *Night of the Pompon* is largely based on her younger sister Merry's lively stories of her misadventures in seventh grade, as well as her own memories of that time. Sarah began to write *Night of the Pompon* when she was an eighteen-year-old freshman in college, studying *The Iliad* and ancient art. "Inspired by a picture of the Athena Parthenos, the statue in the Parthenon, and by a description of the treacherous role Athena played in the hero Hector's death," Sarah explains, "I thought of all the cliques that had existed in my high school and began writing a story about a cult of cheerleaders."

DARK SECRETS™
by Elizabeth Chandler

Who is Megan? She's about to find out....
#1: Legacy of Lies

Megan thought she knew who she was.

Until she came to Grandmother's house.

Until she met Matt, who angered and attracted her as no boy ever had before.

Then she began having dreams again, of a life she never lived, a love she never

knew...a secret that threatened to drive her to the grave.

Home is where the horror is....
#2: Don't Tell

Lauren is coming home, eight years after her mother's mysterious drowning. They said

it was an accident. But the tabloids screamed murder. Aunt Jule was her only refuge,

the beloved second mother she's returning to see. But first Lauren stops at Wisteria's

annual street festival and meets Nick, a tease, a flirt, and a childhood playmate.

The day is almost perfect—until she realizes she's being watched.

A series of nasty "accidents" makes Lauren realize someone wants her dead.

And this time there's no place to run....

Archway Paperbacks
Published by Pocket Books

Jeff Gottesfeld and
Cherie Bennett's

MIRROR IMAGE

When does a dream become a nightmare?
Find out in MIRROR IMAGE as a teenage girl
finds a glittering meteorite, places it under her pillow,
and awakens to discover that her greatest wish
has come true…

STRANGER IN THE MIRROR

Is gorgeous as great as it looks?

RICH GIRL IN THE MIRROR

Watch out what you wish for…

STAR IN THE MIRROR

Sometimes it's fun to play the part

of someone you're not

…until real life takes center stage.

FLIRT IN THE MIRROR

… From tongue-tied girl to the ultimate flirt queen.

From Archway Paperbacks

Published by Pocket Books

2312

Todd Strasser's

Here Comes Heavenly

Here Comes Heavenly

She just appeared out of nowhere. Spiky purple hair, tons of
earrings and rings. Hoops through her eyebrow and nostril,
and tattoos on both arms. She said her name was Heavenly
Litebody. Our nanny. Nanny???

Dance Magic

Heavenly is cool and punk. She sure isn't the nanny our
parents wanted for my baby brother, Tyler. And what's with
all those ladybugs?

Pastabilities

Heavenly Litebody goes to Italy with the family and causes all
kinds of merriment! But...is the land of *amore* ready for her?

Spell Danger

Kit has to find a way to keep Heavenly Litebody, the
Rands' magical, mysterious nanny from leaving the
family forever.

Available from Archway Paperbacks
Published by Pocket Books

2307.01

William Corlett's

THE MAGICIAN'S HOUSE QUARTET

Thirteen-year-old William Constant and his two younger sisters, Mary and Alice, have come to ancient, mysterious Golden House in Wales for the holidays. Their lives will never be the same once they enter the Magician's House—and discover their destiny.

THE STEPS UP THE CHIMNEY
What evil lurks in Golden House? The children know....

William knew something was wrong from the moment they arrived at the railroad station on the border of Wales. First came the stranger who said his name was Steven. "Remember me," he said. Then he vanished. By the time they reached Golden House, even Mary and Alice felt something odd. Who—or what—are the strange animals...a fox, a dog, an owl...that seem to be able to read their minds? Why is it that sometimes the children even see out of the eyes of the animals and hear with their ears? And what is that prickling sensation pulling them toward the secret steps up the chimney? Nothing can stop them as they are drawn deep into the old house, into the realm of the Magician.

THE DOOR IN THE TREE
It's even more dangerous when the magic is real....

It's vacation again—time for William, Mary, and Alice to return to Golden House. They've made a solemn vow not to speak of anything that happened on their last visit to Uncle Jack's home. Was the magic real? It seems like a dream to William and Mary. Only Alice knows the secret of magic: believing. It is Alice who discovers the Dark and Dreadful Path, Alice who is irresistibly drawn into the ancient yew tree. And it is Alice who finds the door in the tree—leading to the secret hiding place of the Magician. *It wasn't a dream!*

Soon they've become the Magician's students, led by the kestrel, the badgers, and the dog into the most perilous assignment of all....

And coming in the fall of 2001:
THE TUNNEL BEHIND THE WATERFALL
THE BRIDGE IN THE CLOUDS

Available from Archway Paperbacks
Published by Pocket Books

3044